THE WORLD HAS PLENTY OF TWELVE-YEAR-OLDS WHO'VE ACCOMPLISHED AMAZING THINGS, LIKE:

Hoisting 308 pounds in one clean lift.

Inventing a braille printer from a Lego set.

Making millions of dollars from candy that's

   good for your teeth.

I wish I could add myself to this list, but I can barely lift a fifty-pound bag of rice, when I play with Legos I usually lose the pieces, and when it comes to candy—especially my favorite kind, with an edible wrapper—I'd rather eat it than sell it.

I do have one hobby I'm not bad at:

Making slime.

Maybe one day I'll make sliming work for me.

All I need is my chance.

ALSO BY MAE RESPICIO

Any Day with You

The House That Lou Built

HOW TO WIN A SLIME WAR

SLIME WAR

MAE RESPICIO

A YEARLING BOOK

Text copyright © 2021 by Mae Respicio
Cover art copyright © 2021 by Nicko Tumamak

All rights reserved. Published in the United States by Yearling, an imprint of
Random House Children's Books, a division of Penguin Random House LLC, New York.
Originally published in hardcover in the United States by Wendy Lamb Books, an imprint of
Random House Children's Books, a division of Penguin Random House LLC, New York, in 2021.

Yearling and the jumping horse design are registered trademarks of Penguin Random House LLC.

Visit us on the Web! rhcbooks.com

Educators and librarians, for a variety of teaching tools, visit us at RHTeachersLibrarians.com

The Library of Congress has cataloged the hardcover edition of this work as follows:
Names: Respicio, Mae, author.
Title: How to win a slime war / Mae Respicio.
Description: First edition. | New York: Wendy Lamb Books, [2021] | Audience: Ages 8–12. |
Audience: Grades 4–6. | Summary: After moving to Sacramento to take over his grandparents'
Filipino market, sixth-grader Alex seeks popularity by selling homemade slime at school, while his
father insists he join a soccer team.
Identifiers: LCCN 2020055499 (print) | LCCN 2020055500 (ebook) | ISBN 978-0-593-30267-5
(hardcover) | ISBN 978-0-593-30268-2 (library binding) | ISBN 978-0-593-30269-9 (ebook)
Subjects: CYAC: Middle schools—Fiction. | Schools—Fiction. | Handicrafts—Fiction. |
Soccer—Fiction. | Stores, Retail—Fiction. | Filipino Americans—Fiction. |
Moving, Household—Fiction.
Classification: LCC PZ7.1.R465 How 2021 (print) | LCC PZ7.1.R465 (ebook) | DDC [Fic]—dc23

ISBN 978-0-593-30270-5 (paperback)

Printed in the United States of America
10 9 8 7 6 5 4 3 2 1
First Yearling Edition 2023

For kid dreamers and doers everywhere

CLASSIC SLIME

1 eight-ounce bottle of white glue
1 tablespoon of baking soda
1/2–2 teaspoons of contact lens solution
A few drops of green food coloring

The world has plenty of twelve-year-olds who've accomplished amazing things, like:

Hoisting 308 pounds in one clean lift.

Inventing a braille printer from a Lego set.

Making millions of dollars from candy that's good
for your teeth.

I wish I could add myself to this list, but I can barely lift a fifty-pound bag of rice, when I play with Legos I usually lose the pieces, and when it comes to candy—especially my favorite kind, with an edible wrapper—I'd rather eat it than sell it.

I do have one hobby I'm not bad at:

Making slime.

I'm stellar at slime challenges. This morning my best friend, Raj, and I are doing one final face-off before my dad and I move from San Jose to Sacramento. It's our way of saying goodbye.

I lay out the ingredients, a couple of bowls, and some fat wooden stirring sticks. Raj sets my laptop on the kitchen counter, raises the volume, and cues up a video:

Slime Time Soraya's 30-Second Challenge!

He rubs his hands together. "I've been waiting the whole week for this!"

We've done all her challenges except this one, which we've been saving for a special occasion.

"Okay, Slime Squad!" Slime Time Soraya says on-screen. "Today we make . . . classic slime! Your goal: mix as *fast* as you can."

"Challenge accepted!" Raj says back.

"Who makes good slime in thirty seconds?" I say. "Art takes much longer than that."

Raj smiles slyly. "You're not the only one with skills, Alex."

We get into position and Soraya counts down:

"Three, two, one . . . GO!"

We squeeze glue into our bowls. Shake in baking soda. Squirt in food coloring. Green, of course.

"Stir, slimers, STIR!"

I mix in quick circles. Raj looks like he's beating eggs. My bowl whirls around, I can't keep it still. The timer ticks loudly and we stir even more frantically.

"Time's up! Sticks down!" she says. We throw down our craft sticks and let out a huge sigh.

I look at Raj—his glasses are covered in drops of green glop—and we burst out laughing. At school I don't have many friends, but I can count on Raj. I'm going to miss him. My dad and I are moving into Lolo and Lola's house, right next door to my cousins, while our grandparents are away on their retirement trip. I'm nervous but excited—Dad and I are taking over Lolo and Lola's Asian market. I've always wanted to have my own business.

Raj scoops up his slime and lifts his stick high. Goop drips down his wrist. "Gross. It didn't congeal at all."

"Told you we needed more time."

There's baking soda on my cheeks and slime hanging from my long hair, too. We take one look at our mess and crack up.

And then Dad walks in.

"Hi, Mr. Manalo." Raj waves but forgets he's still holding his stick. More goo flings on the counter and floor. "Whoops."

"Hey there, Raj." Dad gives him a smile, but it disappears

when he turns my way. "Alex, we're supposed to be packing, not making more work."

"We'll clean it up, Mr. Manalo. We promise," Raj says. He crosses his heart with the stick and accidentally smears goop on his shirt. I try to hold back my laughter. It's lucky Raj is here, otherwise Dad would have gotten mad. He doesn't think sliming's productive (and he hates the cleanup).

Dad nods and goes to do more packing.

"Are you nervous?" Raj asks as we wipe everything down.

"About what?"

"About being the smallest kids in sixth grade!"

Raj and I both got stuck with short genes. I don't remember my mom—she died when I was little—but Dad describes her as petite. He's average height, so out popped me: Alexander T. Manalo, short-kid, science-loving, sports-failing entrepreneurial slimer.

Before I found out about our move, Raj and I decided we would work our way up to the popular table in middle school. He didn't think we could do it. He thought we had to be taller and sportier and way cooler for it to ever happen.

"Why would I be nervous?" I ask as we put everything away. "I'm launching the new me."

"How? By sliming?"

"Don't be so sure, Raj. Things can change."

He snickers, but it makes me think.

It seems impossible that greatness could be achieved by

4

turning glue into goo, but it's happened—Slime Time Soraya and other kids have literally made millions on tutorials and challenges.

Maybe I can, too. Maybe one day I'll make sliming work for me.

All I need is my chance.

SUPER STRETCH

1/2 cup of white glue

3-4 cups of shaving cream

Sprinkle of baking soda

3-4 drops of food coloring

3 squirts of baby oil

Beads, confetti, or any other fun mix-ins

In Lolo and Lola's kitchen, I shake a can of shaving cream and squirt it into a plastic tub, circling until it peaks into a tall, foamy mound. The last time I made this slime Dad got mad since I used his whole can, but he won't miss it. Even though it's been a few weeks since we moved, there are still boxes and packing paper scattered all around.

The glob doesn't look like much until suddenly—it does. Because here's what happens: white glue's a polymer—a molecule with thousands of atoms—and when you combine it with certain ingredients and give it a lot of care, they stick to each other. They turn into something new.

Slime.

I make all kinds: butter slime, crunch slime, sand slime; glow-in-the-dark slime, and one time, an edible batch that tasted like juicy watermelon! Sometimes I create rainbow colors. Other times I plop in teeny beads so it feels unexpected as you're squishing.

There. Finished.

This batch sticks to the bottom of the bowl until I ball it up. I knead it like bread, then pull it like taffy as wide as it'll go—the length of my arms.

I twist it up until it fits neatly into a small, clear container and the bright green shines through.

Hmm. What should I call this?

I write out a label and slap it onto the lid:

Super Stretch.

"Alex! Let's get going!" Dad yells.

I peek my head through the kitchen door. Dad's waiting with a big smile.

"I'll get my helmet," I say.

"How about we drive? There's a box I want to bring home from the store."

"It's okay, I'd rather bike," I say. "Meet ya there?"

Dad nods. I strap on my helmet and head out.

I'm finally getting used to it around here. It's different

from our old home, where we lived in a tall condo on a busy street, surrounded by giant tech companies and endless lines of electric cars whizzing by.

Here I roll past boxy houses with trim lawns.

Past a packed coffee shop, a bustling tire shop.

Past a grassy park of smiley people walking their dogs.

My grandparents' store isn't far from the house. I mean *our* store—I still have to get used to saying that. On the way I stop under a large, leafy oak in the park. Sunlight peeks in through the trees and makes cobwebbed shadows on the pavement.

I stare at a building across the street.

GOLDEN VALLEY MIDDLE SCHOOL

I'll start sixth grade there tomorrow. I'm somewhere between ready . . . and petrified.

My old school had boys twice my height who called me by the wrong name—Allen, Felix, Alec. They made fun of me for "playing with boogers at lunch" when I brought an oozy batch to school. Everyone laughed. We were jealous of the attention people gave them, but mainly we were curious. What was the big fuss about being popular?

Now I start fresh.

I get rolling. In a few minutes I reach a corner of shops. Some boys around my age are biking through the parking lot, too. I wish I had friends to goof off with already.

My family's market is in a little strip mall, along with

a mailbox and shipping place, a nail salon, and an empty storefront with a FOR LEASE sign. Across the way is a similar-looking block but with fancier shops like an olive oil store that sells every flavor of olive oil (why?) and a store that sells unfinished tree stumps (also why?). We've seen lots of businesses come and go, but my family's has been here the longest.

I sling off my helmet, lock up my bike, and push through the glass doors. A bell jingles and a sign says:

NEW AND IMPROVED MANALO MARKET COMING SOON!

This is the whole reason we came here—and I'm ready.

CEO

Sunlight floods the store through floor-to-ceiling windows. Dad grew up in the market, and I've spent a lot of time here, too, while staying with my grandparents on the weekends during school or sometimes the whole summer. Twelve years of the same happy memories: people coming in and out, the smell of savory Filipino food, and a bright mix of languages and laughter. Whenever I walk in I always have the same feeling—of home.

The market has a small seating area and aisles stocked with local and imported food and trinkets from China, Korea, India, Japan, Thailand, and the Philippines. There's a packed, colorful row of candies and crackers, and guava juice boxes that go tastily with salty dried squid snacks. One wall is stacked with pallets of giant rice sacks and has a NO CLIMBING sign. True story: that sign's there because of me and my cousins. It's one of our favorite things to do.

I zoom past the rice wall and smack the bags like drums.

Dad's behind the counter ringing up a mom and her little kid. A small TV plays Filipino soap operas in a steady hum of Taglish—Tagalog words mixed with English. We don't really watch the shows, but since we miss Lola, we keep it on.

"How are your parents doing?" the woman asks my dad.

"Oh, they're loving retirement," he says. "They're in Hawaii now. Then they'll be in Alaska, and back here again for an RV trip up the coast."

The register bings and Dad hands her some change.

"Hold on, don't leave yet," I say to the lady, and I reach under the counter for a small box of candy. I pull one out. It's peach-colored with a clear wrapper, and I hold it up to the boy. "Do you dare me to eat this . . . with the wrapper still *on*?" The kid's eyes widen, and before he can answer I pop it into my mouth. The rice paper melts on my tongue.

"For you," I say, and I hand him the whole box.

"Thanks, guys, see you soon," the mom says, waving, and the doors swing closed.

"Do you know her?" I ask.

Dad shakes his head. "Probably a regular."

Everyone around here loves my grandparents. They trust them. Plus Lolo always gives treats—candies or almond cookies or sweet rice cakes wrapped in banana leaves that Lola bakes—to any cute kid or neighborhood buddy who drops by. "It's never something for nothing, Alex," he likes to say. "Owning a store is about building relationships."

Dad grabs a clipboard and begins roaming the aisles, making notes.

I slide my backpack onto the empty takeout bar, which used to sell fresh, steaming-hot Filipino dishes. We're bringing it back, bigger and better. It's on Dad's list somewhere.

The store stocks everything else, too, all the "normal" items, which some people ask for when they come in. When I ask, "What do you mean by 'normal'?" they say cereal or toilet paper. Seems strange. What we carry *is* normal to people who need it.

Mainly we carry Filipino food: bottles of salty fish sauce and jars of sweet ube, a purple yam, all in neat, bright rows, and a big basket with bags of my favorite Filipino bread, sweet pandesal. The produce section has crates of calamansi, a small green-and-yellow Philippine citrus fruit, plus saba—short, squat bananas that hang like sunshine from hooks.

In the Philippines, Lolo and Lola owned a sari-sari store. It means "variety," although Lola says it means "community." Her favorite memory of running their sari-sari was when everyone in town would come to shop and then stay the whole day chatting and eating, like a family party.

When my grandparents came to California in the 1970s, Lolo wore bell-bottom pants and Lola had fluffy black beehive hair, and they couldn't find anyplace to buy fish sauce—so they opened Manalo Market. It was successful for a long time, but lately it hasn't been doing as well. My grandparents wanted to sell the store and retire, when Dad and I stepped in. We had a family meeting about it.

"We'd like to take over," Dad told my grandparents. "Right, Alex?"

I nodded. I've always wanted to run a business.

Lolo and Lola turned to each other and Lola cried happy tears. Dad worked for a huge tech company that invents apps and other digital things. His sister, my Auntie Gina, runs her family's successful physical therapy clinic. Both of them have always said they never wanted to inherit the market.

"I'm ready for a change," Dad said.

There was more to it, like how Dad broke up with a lady named Revi who I thought might become my stepmom, and how he hated his job staring at computers all day. I liked Revi. The three of us had fun together, and Dad didn't stress out about work when she was around. But I hated his job, too. He worked long hours, and I had a ton of different sitters.

"You've made me very proud, son," Lolo said as they shook on it. No hug, pure business. Dad's not big on hugging.

All morning we hear the store's steady song of the front door jingling and people shopping.

A lola taps on the watermelons and listens close for the perfect hollow sound.

A woman in a suit bags green onions and bok choy, then grabs two Chinese newspapers from a tall stack near the door.

Teenagers giggle and try to steal a pack of gum until Dad gives them his don't-even-try-it look and they pay and say sorry.

Next comes a man I recognize—Paolo, a friend of my grandparents.

"There they are, my favorite Manalos," Paolo says. "But don't tell your lolo I said that."

A dollar bill hangs near the register from our store's first sale, and it's Paolo's. He moved to the neighborhood from Brazil around the same time that my grandparents opened the market. He ate his first Filipino meal here—sticky garlic rice and pork adobo. Once a week he still comes in for lunch and a lottery ticket.

Dad hands him one. "This has lucky written all over it."

Paolo smiles. "What's going on in the empty space next door?"

"No clue yet," Dad says.

Finally the store quiets. Dad goes back to his clipboard. I look through a magazine for young entrepreneurs with people on the cover crossing their arms and staring fiercely into the camera. Someday I'll have CEO after my name. It's my big dream, and my family's always said that a dream's basically the same as a plan.

I take out my slime, unpop the lid, and accidentally spill some near the register.

"Oops," I say.

"Alex! How many times do I have to ask you to be more careful with that stuff?"

Okay. I *may* have a history of letting my product ooze where it shouldn't.

Dad pulls out a container of wet wipes and hands them to me. "Once school gets going, let's figure out some new things for you to get into." He shakes his head.

"Sorry, I'll clean it up," I say.

"Thanks, bud. I'll be in the office for a bit. Holler if you need any help."

I wipe the counter and keep playing, but over a tray this time.

Outside I hear kids yelling. I look, and it's the same pack of boys I saw earlier on their bikes. One of them chains his to a pole and runs right up to the market.

RULE NUMBER ONE

The door chimes and in walks the lone kid. He launches into the first aisle and I can hear the slapping of rice bags. I lose sight of him until he pops up in front of me. Poof! Like magic.

The boy has brown hair and eyes, big front teeth kind of like a gopher. He's staring at my green glob, which I'm poke, poke, poking at.

"What's that?" he asks.

I wonder if he goes to Golden Valley. If we're in the same school I'm not sure what they're into yet, so I don't want to say.

"Nothing special." I lift my slime high and twirl it back into its container. Learned that move online. It's kind of show-offy.

"I've never seen any slime like *that*." He leans way over. His breath smells like tortilla chips. "What brand is it?"

"Why?"

The boy juts out his hand. "Logan O'Grady, nice to meet you." I reach to shake, but he grabs the container.

"Hey!"

"Can I test it out? Please? Slime's my second-favorite thing next to magic! Dude, this is amazing!"

"Next time try asking first," I say, but he grins.

What a weirdo.

"Is it store-bought? Do you carry it here?"

I shake my head. "Nah. I make my own."

"What school do you go to?" he asks.

"Golden Valley."

"Where'd you go before? Golden El? How come I don't know you?"

"We're new here. I'm Alex Manalo."

"What grade?"

"Sixth."

"Same. Just so you know, they're huge on slime at GVM. You've come to the right place, Alex Manalo. Except I should warn you . . . there's a rumor going around."

I raise my eyebrows. "What is it?"

"That last year's sixth graders got in trouble for all their sliming so we're not supposed to bring any to school—like *any*-any—and if we get caught . . . they didn't say what, but I'm guessing something horrible will happen, like we'll get kicked out . . . or we'll have to help pass out hot lunch or something. But we'll see about that." He smushes the slime back into its case. "Wow! Very professional! How much?"

"How much what?"

"How much do you charge? Meadow MacPhearson upped her prices, so I'd rather buy yours—that girl needs some real competition. Last year everyone was too scared to sell against her, or if they tried . . . let's just say it didn't work out well for them." My eyes widen. "It'd be nice to have more options."

"I don't sell my slime."

"Then why do you make it?"

"Because . . . I like to?"

"Alex, let's go over the rules of GVM. Rule number one: make slime, sell slime." He shakes his head. "Duh."

"Do *you* sell slime?" I ask.

He studies me up and down like he's trying to figure me out. "Nope. Maker's not my thing"—the corners of his mouth turn up—"but *seller* could be."

I shove the container back into his hands. "Here ya go, Logan, on the house."

"Hey, thanks!" He stuffs it into his pocket. "Wanna see a trick?"

He shows me his palms—one has a shiny quarter. He balls both hands into fists, shakes them in the air, and when he opens—the quarter's gone.

Not bad.

I tried to learn magic by watching tutorials online, but I couldn't get the hang of it. I clicked on a sliming video instead, and that's when I got hooked.

"How'd you do that?" I ask.

Logan grins. "I don't know about magic, but I got a couple of Twix up my sleeves." He stretches his arms toward me and two thin chocolate bars peek out at the wrists. I laugh. Okay, maybe I like this guy.

"Cool, thanks." I grab one and take a bite.

"Oh, I guess I need to pay you for the chocolate, huh?" he mumbles, and fishes out some dollars, his own Twix hanging out of his mouth. "For these, too." He plonks down a handful of creamy, milky White Rabbit—another delicious candy where the inner wrapper melts in your mouth.

Talk about magic—I didn't even see him grab any of that stuff. He's good.

Those boys on their bikes walk past the window, shoving each other and snickering. Logan stares at them. "Think about what I said, okay? About selling slime." And like that he's out the door, shouting, "Guys, wait up!" The glass swings behind him and he folds easily into their pack.

Dad comes in carrying a big gray plastic tub.

"Was that a customer? I heard voices."

"Just some kid."

Dad sets the tub down. "There's no better feeling than

being your own boss and making things happen, Alex." He beams at me. "Ready to close up?"

I nod and go over to the door. Through the glass I see Logan and those boys riding away.

I flip the sign from OPEN to CLOSED.

NOW IT'S YOUR TURN

At home I hang my helmet on a hook next to the Shrine. It's what Dad and Auntie Gina call the big wood-and-glass case in the living room that protects all their accomplishments: sports trophies, debate team ribbons, diplomas, and framed pictures of them getting those awards. Dad has the most, with shiny golden guys from every sport he's ever played. The trophies twinkle when the lights bounce off them. Sometimes I wonder how he got so athletic when my grandparents aren't. And sometimes I think he wonders why I'm not athletic like him.

Dad's at the dining table digging through a box. "Ah, here it is." He pulls out my one and only trophy—an engraved bronze plaque that says:

ALEX MANALO

SILICON VALLEY KIDPRENEUR

OF THE YEAR!

"I've seen you eyeing the Shrine, and it's about time we added this." He swings open the doors and finds a spot. "Now that you're starting middle school, we can give you your own shelf to rack up the awards, huh?" It seems like he's trying to joke, but I know he means it.

Manalo is a common last name in the Philippines. It means "to win." But in twelve years, I've only ever known how it feels to win once, and that was when I did Kidpreneur. For a whole week we got to learn savvy business skills and competed in contests for plaques and bragging rights. During the final challenge we had to invent a product and come up with a business plan, and mine won. Personalized mouth guards.

I'd had the idea for a while, and when I did my market research I couldn't find any schools or sports teams that used them. Since people love to brag about themselves, a mouth guard with your name on it seemed perfect. *And* my invention was something as close to sports as possible, which I knew would make Dad happy. I was right. He let me rent a 3D printer and I made a prototype—it cinched my win. I got rock star status, an interview on the local news, and an announcement in the school bulletin. Even the popular kids who normally didn't talk to me asked all about it, although I didn't get invited to sit with them.

Winning still felt fantastic, and Dad threw an actual party. He blew up balloons and uncorked sparkling cider, and we celebrated at a nice restaurant, where he introduced me to all the waiters as Alex Manalo, Future CEO.

I vowed to myself I'd win at something again—I loved how much Dad got into it—but I'm not sure at what yet. Looks like Dad's waiting for the same thing.

He closes the door to the Shrine and I head upstairs. "Hey, buddy, there's something I want to talk about," he says.

"Can we do it later? Raj and I are about to play online."

"It'll only take a second. I have something special to share with you."

On the dining table sits that bin he brought back from the market. I join him and he pulls out goalie gloves, shin guards, balled-up socks . . .

Soccer gear?

"That equipment looks kind of old," I say.

"It is. I can't believe your grandparents kept all this. Pretty cool." He lifts out a black-and-white ball, worn and dirty but still inflated, and spins it on his finger. "You know how many goals I scored with this?"

I roll my eyes.

"Well, Alex, now it's your turn."

He tosses the ball my way and I block it so I don't get hit. It bounces and rolls.

"My turn for what?" He knows I'm horrible at soccer—at all sports.

"I signed us up for the local rec league. I'll coach, you'll play. A team of our own. What do you think?"

"Our own?"

"Yeah! It'll be good for you to go outside, instead of being holed up in your room making that . . . slime."

"Sliming's an art. Art's good, too," I say.

"Sure, but you need more well-rounded hobbies. Physical ones. *Real* ones. We have to start thinking about high school—maybe toughen you up a bit, have you finally get a haircut." He smiles and tousles my hair. I've had longish hair the past few years. It's not short like my cousins Nick and Sammy's. No special reason why, I just like it this way.

"Ummm . . . ," I say. I'd rather do anything else: *Dungeons & Dragons*, Media Club, even Math Brigade. Whatever doesn't involve sticks or balls or kids flying at me.

"Well?"

I reach for the ball and throw it at the bin, but it hits the rim and bounces. "I don't know."

"Could be fun. We haven't done anything together since Cub Scouts."

That was third grade. Dad's not a nature guy, but he loved that we got to sell things for fundraisers. We made a solid team, and Dad was determined for us to outsell everyone else.

"Did you and Lolo ever play a sport together?" I ask.

Dad shakes his head. "He was busy all the time with

the store, but he liked watching sports on TV—and shouting at the screen." This makes us both laugh. Lolo's still loyal to every local team and owns multiple San Francisco Giants hats.

"If I decide not to play, will you still coach?"

"I'd like us both to make the commitment, Alexander. We moved so we could spend more quality time together, remember?"

Not like this, I want to say, but the smile on his face stretches so wide I don't want to disappoint him.

I don't know why soccer's so important to my dad. I've got things important to me, too.

He's studying my face, maybe trying to hypnotize me into saying yes.

Finally I say, "I'll think about it."

"That's all I ask, Alex. Thank you."

The ball rolled over to my feet. I throw it at the bin—but miss. Again. He scoops it up and with one aim tosses it in.

* * *

Upstairs I flip open my laptop and check if Raj is online.

I wish Dad could be happy with the things I like. I've tried lots of ways to make him proud. I joined student council as marketing manager. He said, "You didn't want to run for president?" I tried to break a world record by eating only one color of food in twenty-four hours—orange. I figured I could start off with nachos, but he didn't seem impressed. Last year I almost got straight As—except for a B-minus in math—and he said, "I'll get you a tutor!"

But the school play, my band concert when I had a trumpet solo, the field trip where we got to read to dogs at the library—the things that really mattered to me—he never made it. Auntie Gina and my grandparents would go in his place. They'd remind me that my dad worked hard because the Bay Area is so darn expensive, which meant sacrifice, and it's what Lolo had to do when Dad was growing up and blah-blah-blah-yeah-yeah-yeah.

I slip on my headset. "Anybody there?" I say. Raj must have not logged on yet, but my phone buzzes. It's a text from Raj, a selfie of him with some of the boys who used to make fun of us. Looks like they're in a courtyard eating lunch with kids in the background, a few I recognize from my old school. The boys have grins so wide, making silly faces at the camera. His text says:

Sorry, can't play. But look what happened!

Wow. Raj actually did it.

I slip my headphones off. I'm not going to have a single friend to sit with during lunch at my new school. My chest tightens as I think about having to be on my own. But as I stare at Raj's picture, it's like he's encouraging me. If he did it, I can, too.

THERE HE IS

First day of sixth grade.

I glance at my watch. It's analog, not some fancy one that counts my steps or talks to me when I call out its name. It's old and belonged to Lolo. Whenever I felt nervous about something, he'd hold it up to my ear and ask me to close my eyes, and I'd listen to the second hand tick. Like a heartbeat. Lolo gave the watch to Dad; then Dad gave it to me—that was Lolo's plan all along. He always says to know myself is to know what and who came before us. Kind of like the market, a special thing that threads us together.

I'm about to be late—I hop onto my bike. Jitters have landed like aliens in the pit of my stomach. But the harder I pedal, the faster they can go back into outer space and I can calm down.

In front of Golden Valley Middle is a large crosswalk bustling with cars and bikers and students. An older grandma type in a fluorescent yellow vest holds her hands up to us kids to stop, and we wait for the traffic to clear. I get off my bicycle and pull a container of slime out of my pocket. Maybe playing with it will help my nerves settle.

There's a girl waiting next to me. She's wearing a sparkly backpack, the expensive kind that some kids at my last school wanted and would squeal over. Normally I don't care about what's "in" or what I'm wearing, but I know kids who want whatever brands they see online or on TV. I wonder if they'll be like that here.

The girl's gaze lands on my slime, and I think she's trying to read the label. Then I remember what Logan said about how last year's sixth graders got in trouble for all their sliming. I stuff the container into my back pocket, and now the girl looks at me.

Once again the aliens have landed. I tighten my grip on the handlebars.

"Where'd you get that slime?" she asks. "Did you buy it from someone here?"

I shake my head. "I made it," I say.

She eyes me, then glares.

Our old neighborhood had kids from families whose parents made millions inventing things like apps that Dad thought actually make people's lives more stressful. Raj said at least when I moved I wouldn't have to go to school with snooty rich tech kids, but he hasn't seen this girl.

Cars whiz down the long street, and as the light turns

red, the crossing guard walks into the middle of the road, raises her stop sign, and thunders: "Awesome kids crossing! Thank you!" She waves me on. "New here?"

I nod and she smiles. "Got a name?"

"Alex Manalo."

"Manalo? No kidding! I know your grandparents. I'm the one who taught Nick how to knit—did he ever tell you that? I'm Ellie. You'll see me here every school day, rain or shine." Her kind face makes me want to smile back. I think Ellie owned the day care my cousins went to, and I'm pretty sure I've seen her at the market. "And welcome back, Marvelous Meadow!" she says to Backpack Girl, and the girl's sour expression morphs into sweet.

"Ellie! I made a special batch for your grandkids. I even named it after you! The Elastic Ellie!" The girl hands something to Ellie, who belts out a raspy chuckle.

"Nice! But remember not to play with slime at school, you got me?"

Slime?

Maybe that kid Logan at the store was right.

I try to see what kind of slime Backpack Girl threw to Ellie, but she scrunches her nose like she's whiffed something awful. "What are *you* looking at?" she says, brushing past me.

Sheesh. Whatever.

At the racks in front of school I slip my bike in and pull

out a crumpled paper with my locker number and first-period classroom. I find my locker, spin a code onto the wheel, and swing the door open. From my backpack I pull out Super Stretch and undo the lid. I poke my finger in it. *Pop. Pop. Pop.* Adding a smidge of baby oil does that. My nerves feel soothed.

"There he is," a voice says. It's that Logan kid. A girl is with him.

"I'm Kendra," she says, handing me some dollar bills.

"What's this for?" I ask.

"She wants to buy your slime," Logan whispers into my ear.

"Yeah, I was testing out Logan's. How'd you get it so elasticky? I've never had any that stretched so far."

"I've been slime-sperimenting."

"I'll take one," she says. I keep waiting for her to say *Just kidding!* but she shakes the money in my face. "Come on! Before they catch us!"

"Who?" I say.

"The teachers," Logan whispers.

Kendra glances around. "Do we have a deal or not?"

Logan grabs her money and stuffs it into my hand.

"I've already used this batch and I don't have any more," I say.

"Then bring some tomorrow," Logan says. "She knows where to find you."

"Cool, thanks," Kendra says, and she runs off.

Logan grins. "You *have* to start selling, Alex. I can help. I already know all the ins and outs here—who buys what, which teachers go where. Face it, we were meant to help each other."

I look at him skeptically. "Why would you want to help me?"

"Easy. For fifty percent!" He grabs two of the bills and pushes them into his pocket. I'm left with the rest and a promise to some girl that I didn't make. I'll find Kendra later and give her money back. "What's your first class?" Logan asks, and I show him my paper. "Mine too. Let's go."

THE SCIENCE OF SLIME

I follow Logan into first-period science. Our classroom seems interesting: 3D planets hang from the ceiling, counters with beakers and computers line the walls, and tall lab tables fit two kids each. Logan finds a seat with someone he knows. The classroom pings with energy and a jittery jolt zooms through me.

One table's empty, so I take a seat. I sit on my hands to keep them from shaking.

Students keep filing in, and I wait for somebody to sit next to me, but I keep getting passed by. The girl from the crosswalk, Meadow, comes in, too, and sits a few rows up.

I glance down at my paper to make sure I'm in the right room—the young, perky woman walking around the class doesn't seem like a Mr. Butzer. When I got my schedule, Dad saw *Butzer* listed and said, "Wow, Mr. B's still there? He must be a thousand years old. He always kept things interesting."

The woman glances my way. Quietly, I ask, "Is this science with Mr. Butzer?" A few kids across the aisle must hear me, I think, because they laugh.

"I was *Miss* Butzer but I turned into Mrs. Graham over the summer, which was very fortunate because you try growing up with the word *butt* in your name." She smiles. "Mr. Butzer is my dad. He's retired now. They must have forgotten to change the name on the slip."

"Oh," I say. "My dad had your dad as his teacher."

"He did? Who's your father?" I tell her my name and his—John Manalo.

"What a fun coincidence! Your dad played soccer in high school with my older brother! He was amazing, but I'm sure you know." She grins. "I'm very glad to have you in class, Alex." Mrs. Graham walks to the front of the room and clears her throat. "All right, friends, good morning! The bell has rung and I love seeing all this excitement!"

I expected someone boring, but she flings off her blazer, and her shirt has a periodic elements table and the words: I WEAR THIS PERIODICALLY.

A little cringey, but I'll give her a chance.

She's about to say something but then goes over to a boy sitting in front of Logan, who's pounding a bright blue blob of slime on the glossy black table. Kids next to him giggle as he stretches it out; one girl pokes at the goo. None of them notices our teacher—until she puts out her hand and the boy looks up, guiltily. The whole class turns quiet.

"I'm sure you know the rules, Mr.—?"

"Davis. Trevor Davis."

He plops the glob and its container into her palm.

Mrs. Graham walks around the room now, a glint in her eyes. "Sixth graders, why don't slugs need shells to protect themselves?"

Silence.

"Volunteers?"

I look around. *Should I?*

At my old school we had one teacher who made everyone feel scared and embarrassed if they gave the wrong answer—maybe that's why no one's answering?

Slowly I raise my hand. Logan catches my eyes and discreetly shakes his head.

"I'm glad to see you jumping right in, Mr. Manalo. Okay, tell me. Why don't slugs have shells to protect themselves?"

"Because of . . . slime?" I say.

"Affirmative!" she yells. "And what, budding scientists, drips out of your nose when you're sick?

"Nasty stuff!" Logan shouts.

"Bingo!" she says. "Or, more precisely, mucus. And why do our bodies make it?" Still, no hands up. "It's because we need it *to survive*. Slimy mucus helps our bodies get rid of bacteria that makes us sick."

"If that's true, Logan must be the healthiest person alive because he's always got boogers," says the boy whose slime got confiscated. Meadow laughs. Logan rolls his eyes like it doesn't bother him.

"I will not tolerate that type of talk in my classroom, Mr. Davis."

"Sorry, Mrs. Graham," he says.

She nods at him. "Now what does this all mean? Come on, come on, slime is of the essence!" she says. "Mr. Manalo, care to guess?"

I was okay with raising my hand when I knew the answer, but I hate getting put on the spot. My cheeks feel warm.

"Umm . . . you . . . really, *really* like slime?" I say, and some kids snicker.

Mrs. Graham whips around, grabs a marker, and writes on the board without stopping, like she's in a hurry, and when she reaches the end taps hard dots onto all her exclamation points.

The Science of Slime!!!!!!!!!

"For our very first unit, we'll learn about slime in the natural world, and at the end, you'll make some of your own as homework and bring it into class. Bonus: you'll get the period to play with it to your heart's content." She smiles and the class cheers. "This will be paired with an essay you'll be required to write and several pop quizzes over the next few weeks." The class boos.

I'm into it. All of it.

She hands Trevor back his slime. "Look, kids, some real

talk. We're still getting acquainted, but I already know how much you love sliming. I designed this unit as a way to make your passion work. However, no slime in class, is that clear? Same with cell phones and other distractions."

Toward the end of class, a little wadded ball of paper hits my neck.

I look around and Logan smiles at me. He points to the clock, raises three fingers, and puts each one down in time with the ticking hand.

Three ... two ... one ...

The bell blares and everyone packs up in a frenzy.

More classes and more questions, and more empty chairs next to mine. Until, finally, lunchtime.

MY TURF

In the courtyard kids are already hunched in clusters talking and eating at their tables. I walk through and manage to find one without a single person, so I plop myself there and dig out my lunch bag. Auntie Gina packed it—turkey on wheat, no mayo. She came over last night to make sure I felt ready for today.

When I think of what a mom would be like, I always think of my aunt. She was my mom's best friend. Every year on Mom's birthday, Auntie shares old pictures and stories: of Mom twirling onstage during her college dance days, or taking care of her lush orchid garden, or how even though Dad was popular in high school, Mom could care less. Mom was like a rainbow, she brought color to things and made everyone happy. Her job was running a community center, and every year she planned a neighborhood festival full of life and laughter.

Most of the things I know about my mom come from

Auntie or from Nanang and Tatang—Mom's parents, who live in Hawaii. Dad doesn't talk about her much, but I wish he would.

I take a chewy bite of my sandwich.

"Hey! New Kid!" I hear, and it's Logan waving me over, sitting with two other people, a boy who wears a velvety black cape and has a magic wand by his side, and a girl whose face is half hidden by a book. My feet feel glued, but I manage to grab my stuff and join them.

"Hey," I say.

"This is Alex, the guy I told you about!" Logan introduces me first to Carl Copperfield, and goes on to tell me that they do YMCA Magic Club together. Carl's name is really Carl Franklin, but his stage name, and what he goes by to his friends, matches his favorite magician.

"Watch carefully," Carl says.

He shows me a coin in his palm before closing his hand and tapping it with the white tip of his wand. When he opens, the coin's gone. Now Logan shows me *his* empty palm, which he balls up. Carl taps it with his wand.

"Voilà!" Logan says, and when he opens his fist—the coin appears.

"Wow!" I say.

The girl laughs. "They've been practicing that since the second-grade talent show." She puts down what she's reading—*The Richest Man in Babylon*—takes one of my hands with both of hers, and shakes vigorously. "I'm Pepper. Pleasure to finally meet you, Alex."

"Looks like an interesting book," I say.

"It is! My parents own a bookstore, so I have the world's knowledge at my fingertips!" She beams.

Pepper's taller than all of us and wears braces, a red beanie, and a huge smile that takes up her whole face.

"Nice," I say. She must know something about business, then.

"I have to see if Logan was right," Pepper says. She lays out her palm. "Slime me." It's kind of nice getting sliming attention when at my last school people made fun of it. I give her the teeny tub of this morning's batch. She snaps off the lid and gently shakes the container. "Proper wiggle."

Another kid walks by, holds up two dollars, and says, "I want in."

Logan grabs the container from Pepper, secures the top, and hands it to the boy, who gives Logan some money and takes off.

"Hey, that's not fresh slime!" I say.

"That's why I only charged him half." Logan hands me a dollar and pockets the other. "You made the right choice to partner up, Alexander."

The only time I ever hear my full name is when I'm in trouble with Dad, like last year when kids on the bus threw spit wads and I joined in—only because everyone else did it.

"I go by Alex," I say.

Pepper grins. "Good. It's a catchier slimer name." I nod. She's smart.

"Well, Alex, you just got another sale." Logan motions to a packed courtyard. "Take a look around. You could be *sixth-grade famous.*"

More kids approach asking to test my slime and wanting to know what school I came from. Some even tell me they've shopped at Manalo Market. Word about me spread—outside of Kidpreneur, that's never happened.

One table of boys keeps looking our way until someone walks by them with toilet paper trailing from his shoe and they point and hoot obnoxiously. Trevor sits in the middle doing all the talking while the others high-five. There's a redheaded kid next to him, and they look like the leaders. I notice how everyone at all the other tables in the courtyard looks Trevor's way.

I've always wanted to be the kid everyone's watching.

"Who's that Trevor person from science?" I ask Logan.

"My best friend since preschool," he says. "Until today." He frowns.

"Why? What happened?"

Logan shrugs. "I don't know. He made all these new friends over the summer, like that kid Rudy sitting next to him, and now . . . he's just different. Trevor used to be nice." Logan looks away. I think about Raj and the picture he sent me. I wonder how I would have felt if we were still in sixth grade together but he was making all new friends without me.

Out of the corner of my eye, I see a girl charging up to us.

"Ugh. What does she want?" Logan says.

The girl stops at our table and her eyes bore into mine. It's Meadow.

"I knew something was up when I saw you this morning," she says, looking right at me. "What do you think you're doing?"

"Leave him alone, Meadow," Logan says, and she zaps her attention toward him.

"My school, my slime." She crosses her arms.

Logan jumps up and fans a dollar in front of her face. "And who gave *you* reign?"

"Pipe down," Meadow says. "You know how the yard duties are."

I look from Logan to Meadow and it's like they're having a stare-off. "Hey, guys, whatever this is I don't want to get in the middle, okay?" I try to say in an even tone. Entrepreneurs have to stay calm because they never know what might pop up—when you're starting a business, anything can happen.

Meadow takes a step closer to me and puts her fists on her hips. "Do you even know who I am?"

"Alex Manalo, Meadow MacPhearson. You were bound

to meet at some point." Logan bites into his sandwich and very nonchalantly says, "Why isn't a ham sandwich called a hamwich? There's an opportunity there."

"You tell this new kid he can't just come in here and start selling slime on *my turf*!" Even though she said not to, she's the one yelling now.

A mob of looky-loos has grown around us.

"*Your* turf? Says who? We're not in fifth grade anymore, Meadow," Logan says. "New school, new rules. Why do you get to hog it all?"

Meadow stares at Logan. Sure, smooth, and steely-eyed, she says: "Slime War. Me and your new-kid friend."

"You're on!" Logan sticks out his hand and they shake.

I have no idea what just went down.

I scan the crowd for clues: some kids watch us with wide eyes, some still eat, some erupt into laughter. One kid stuffs popcorn into his mouth from a plastic baggie like he's at the movies and we're the show.

I shake my head. "What's a Slime War?"

Logan leans in. "I'll explain later."

"This is how it's gonna work—" Meadow begins, but Logan holds up a hand.

"*You* can't make the rules. That's not fair and you know it."

Meadow looks from Logan to me. "Fine." She snaps at a girl next to her, who rises to attention. "Kristina B."

Logan shakes his head. "Kristina B.'s *your* party. If we're going to do this fair and square, we need someone neutral."

Meadow and Logan glance around.

Logan points to a tall tree across the courtyard, where there's a boy in an old-timey gray vest, suspenders, and a polka-dot bow tie leaning against a sprawling oak, digging into a cup of chocolate pudding. He licks his spoon clean.

He's eyeing us.

Logan says to Meadow: "Him."

Meadow replies: "Perfect."

LEGEND OF THE SLIME

Bow Tie Kid strides toward our table without anyone calling him over. Casually, he chucks his empty pudding container into the trash can and misses, but some boy scampers behind to pick it up and throw it into the compost bin.

He walks with his hands in his pockets and so, so smoothly, like he's on wheels. He glides over to our table. Kids part to make an opening.

Now that's a grand entrance.

"I have been observing you all, and we could have settled this negotiation much sooner. However, I am happy to step in."

He looked more impressive from farther away. Up close he's got zits and is shorter than I am—but he oozes confidence. The crowd's mesmerized. He could be selling snake oil and I don't think anyone would care.

"You. New Kid," he says.

I wish they'd stop calling me that—I've got a name. "It's Alex Manalo."

"Okay, Felix." Great. Someone else who can't get my name right. He's still looking right at me. "Do you know and accept the legend of the slime?"

Logan whispers: "That's Melvin Moore and he makes the rules. *Eighth grader.*" I nod.

"No, what is it?" I say to Melvin.

"Listen closely and I shall explain, Felix Slimanalo." Melvin steps onto a bench, cracks his knuckles, and clears his throat.

"Legend has it that many years ago, before the age of online enslimemenment, there existed two sixth-grade slimers at Golden Valley Middle School in the Central Valley of California, who separately decided to make and sell slime. They followed their passion *and* they followed it well.

"However, what they did not expect was that their individual sliming efforts would cause a great divide at this very school. Sixth graders were torn between the two camps. Allegiances were made. Tears were shed. Slime was spilled." The crowd gasps. Spilled slime is tragic. They must know the story, but Melvin smiles and continues.

"And so it came to pass that the first Slime War would begin. It was decided that the two slimers would battle, and the winner would take territory, which meant controlling all sliming activity here, on our beloved school grounds, for the remainder of their middle school years.

"And that winner, my friends . . . was Slime Time Soraya."

The crowd gasps again. Whispers bounce around as kids

glance at each other—me included. *Everyone* has heard of Slime Time Soraya, a true legend who went on to fame and fortune because of her innovative and expert sliming techniques. I had no idea she went *here*. So cool.

Melvin Moore continues: "You heard me right, my friends—Queen Slime Time Soraya, the first kid ever to create her own onslime channel, which would eventually amass billions of views and followers, get multiple worldwide sponsorships, and be mentioned at every Slime War across this great universe!

"Nevertheless, as fads often go, sliming at Golden Valley Middle School died down as other trends arose: fidget spinners, bottle flipping, and the nonsensical activity of box opening. There has not been a Slime War since the time of Soraya, although legend reveals that if our fine school were ever again to be divided by slime, a new war should take place. Legend also has it that whoever wins the next Slime War will inherit the Slime Time Soraya Spell of Good Fortune: massive riches and becoming leader of their own slime empire."

He steps down and walks in between everyone.

"It starts here. At Golden Valley. With the Slime War. We shall carry on this legend!"

Melvin Moore stands between me and Meadow and yanks our arms high—kids cheer.

"I hereby declare a Slime War!"

He finishes with a bow, bending low at the knees and flourishing his arms.

Kristina B. steps in front of Meadow, and Logan steps in front of me. Kristina B. says, "On behalf of Meadow MacPhearson, we accept the legend of the Slime War."

Logan steps in front of me. "On behalf of Alex Manalo, we accept the legend of the Slime War."

Logan and Kristina B. shake.

"Wait a second!" I blurt out, but it's too late, their hands are gripped. Kids around us nod their heads like it's a done deal—even though I'm not sure what any of this means.

"Slimers, shake," Melvin says. Meadow shoves out her greasy hand. She probably doesn't even wash or use sanitizer after sliming the way a good slimer should.

I stare at her palm. Everyone's waiting.

Meadow taps her foot like it's a windup toy. "You scared of a little *goo*?"

I look around, give my new schoolmates a smile, then stare Meadow right in the face.

I jut out my palm.

She grabs it and tightens her grip, her knuckles whitening, like she'll squeeze my hand off. Her lips move into a straight line as tight as a string. If I pulled it, she'd explode.

The bell rings, Meadow drops my hand, and everyone scatters. Only Logan and me are left.

"What just happened?" I ask.

"Dude, that was incredible. Our grade needs you for this. Meadow's been bullying everyone so she can be the only person to sell slime at school. Meadow—and kids like her—they already have everything, it's not fair."

"So she's got the monopoly?" I say. He looks at me funny. "You know, when only one person is the supplier."

"First Mrs. Graham's questions and now this?" Logan says.

"I took business lessons."

"Good. Then I know for sure you can help us. If you win, it means we're out of her control—no more Meadow's Monopoly. We'll set up our business, sell every day, and everyone will know us."

"You're right. We won't be the little guys," I say, remembering how Raj and I felt last year. "Because *we'll* represent them."

"*We'll* be the heroes," he says.

We smile at each other.

"Whip up more slime and bring it tomorrow for our first day of sales," Logan tells me. "I'll do the rest."

Trevor, Rudy, and those boys from earlier saunter by and snicker. "You guys don't stand a chance," Rudy says. Trevor laughs and gives his friend a fist bump.

Logan turns to me and I shake my head. "Let's prove them wrong."

I'm so in.

SLIMY McFLUFF

2 cups of cornstarch

1 cup of hair conditioner in your
favorite scent

5 drops of food coloring

It's happening! My own business!

Let's. Go.

I have so many ideas that if I don't get them out this second I'll lose them.

I bolt into the store, yelling, "Hi, Dad! Bye, Dad!" as I rush past to the back kitchen. I've got a secret stash of ingredients for whenever I get bored. I pull them out, measure everything into a silver bowl, mix quickly, and add drops of water until it's the right amount of fluff.

This batch needs to feel like a cloud.

I squish the slime on a tray. This kind will be a

crowd-pleaser—it's smooth like ocean rocks. I'm going to make all types.

The rules for the Slime War are simple:

- Each team has one week to sell.
- Both teams will charge the same price.
- Sell as much as we can.
- Winner sells most.
- Don't get caught.

Meadow and I and our teams will sell through next Monday, exactly a week from now. Then Melvin Moore, as the neutral party, will total our profits and announce the winner. If my slime wins, Logan and I take the school back.

I finish up my batch and wash my hands. Out in the storeroom, two girls wander the candy aisle, showing each other packages and saying things like *Oh yum, this one's my favorite!* One of the girls, wearing overalls with a strap hanging down her back, carries a shopping basket loaded with all the seriously good stuff. Her friend goes over to the rice wall and slaps the bags.

They both watch me, then whisper to each other. I've never seen these girls before, but they keep looking over.

"Umm . . . hi?" I finally say.

They walk up to me. "You're Alex," says the girl in the overalls. "I'm Kristina T." She points to her friend. "This is Robin."

Now they're both staring. The other girl looks me up and down. She shakes her head and says to her friend, "I don't know. A lot of people have tried. How can *he* do it?"

"Standing right here," I say, with a little wave.

"I tried to sell slime against Meadow once, but I totally failed." Robin nods. "She's got a lot of good tricks, you know," Kristina T. says.

"Tricks?" I say.

Both girls eye me now. "I don't know if you've got the sliming touch," says Robin.

Dad's in the corner unboxing some new inventory, and I don't want him to hear. He can't know about this yet, not until the perfect moment. He'll think the Slime War is a waste of time.

"We'll just have to see, right?" I say.

"Come on, let's go pay," Kristina T. says. They go to the front and dump their loot on the counter—different-flavored jellies; long, thin cookie sticks half covered in chocolate; and chewy bites of bean-filled mochi balls—and Dad rings them up with a friendly smile.

"I love these jellies," Robin says. "This is the only place right by school where we can find them." She grabs one— a little plastic cup the size of her thumb—peels off the paper top, slurps it up, and licks her lips. Lychee-flavored. These girls have good taste.

I help Dad put everything into a bag and hand it to them.

"Enjoy, kiddos," he says, but they stand there, waiting. "Yes? You need something else?"

"The old owner used to give us those candies where you can eat the wrapper," Kristina T. says.

"For free," Robin says.

I take out the box. They grab a couple and leave.

"Good to see you meeting people already," Dad says. "Since you're on your bike, you want to head home now? I'll be leaving in a couple minutes." I nod.

I can't believe those kids know my name. My mouth turns up. Everyone at school will know who I am once I show them how to win a Slime War.

CATCH IT

I make it home as Auntie Gina and my cousin Nick pull into their driveway. Their family lives next door—another reason Dad wanted to move back was so I could have my cousins around. Nick's in high school, tenth grade, and his brother, Sammy, is a junior.

Auntie pops the trunk and takes out brown grocery bags.

"Hey, sweetie," she says. "Thought I'd help you bachelors out. I know your dad hasn't had time to do much of this lately. Can you help me carry everything in, please?" I grab some bags, she gives me a kiss on the forehead, and we cross the lawn to my grandparents' house.

"How was the clinic today?" I ask, pushing the door open. We step inside.

"Busy, busy, busy!" she says.

Auntie Gina is my dad's sister, and she does a ton for our whole family. Right now she's helping us organize all of Lolo and Lola's store files as we get ready to remodel.

Auntie's married to Uncle Benny, and they own a physical therapy clinic—Uncle's a physical therapist and Auntie runs everything and grows their business. She went to business school like Dad, and like I probably will one day. Their clinic treats all kinds of patients, even famous hockey players from the Sactown Slick Sticks. At the clinic's tenth-anniversary party, Auntie Gina made two announcements: First, they'd had their most successful year ever. Second, the Slick Sticks had decided to use them as their official PT clinic. Coloma Physical Therapy was named one of the top local businesses in the state.

Lola shrieked, everyone laughed, and Uncle Benny turned to me and said: "See, Alex? We're just as important to hockey players as dentists are." Then he grinned—with a piece of spinach he stuck on his tooth to make it look missing. I couldn't stop laughing. It's what eventually gave me my idea for personalized mouth guards. Inspiration can spark from anywhere and everywhere.

Auntie, Nick, and I unload groceries in the kitchen. When we're done, Nick says to me, "Let's go shoot some hoops."

"Nah, I'm good."

He throws me a ball the way Dad does—hard and without warning. What's with that? I shield my face instead of trying to catch it.

"No you're not," he says. "C'mon."

"Fine."

Nick loves soccer as much as Dad, but he loves knitting, too. His brother, Sammy, used to make fun of him for it—until he knit a funny red-and-green Santa sweater for their Chihuahua, Choop, and now he's always asking Nick to make more. Choop has a sweater for every holiday, including a menacing Darth Vader one he wears every fourth of May so we can all say: "May the Fourth Be with You!"

We head for the cul-de-sac, where the same hoop has stood since Dad was a kid.

Nick aims and shoots. The ball bounces off the rim and doesn't make it in.

Nick and Sammy are both star athletes and straight-A students—the way Dad was at their age—and every bit hulked and bulked like they could knock scrawny me down with a light tap on my shoulder. But they treat me like a brother, always have.

I'm thinking of telling Nick about the Slime War when Dad pulls into our driveway and gets out.

"Hey, Uncle!" Nick shouts. "Guess what? I made varsity soccer!"

Dad's eyes light up. "What? As a sophomore? Amazing, Nick!"

My cousins make my life easier because they can be the sports sons Dad's always wanted. Most of the time it doesn't bother me since it gets him off my case, except when he starts going on and on about what solid players they are.

Nick fetches the ball and passes it my way. "Your turn."

I dribble once, twice, three times and shoot. It hits the rim, too, and bounces over to Dad.

"Gotta work on your aim, son," he says. He throws the ball and it swooshes in, barely making a sound. "See? Easy."

Nick's eyes meet mine. He knows how Dad gets sometimes.

"Hey, boys, dinner soon," Auntie bellows from the doorway. "Pizza night!"

"Be right there," Nick says. He's still looking at me, like he feels bad—until he slaps my shoulder and shouts, "Race you!"—and we both make it to the door. I touch the handle seconds before he does and we bust up. He probably let me win, he always does, but I never care because we always have a blast when we're hanging out. I'd play soccer with Dad if it could feel the same way.

I'M GOOD AT MAKING THINGS

Nick and I set the table and I hear the happy jumble of Sammy and Uncle Benny coming in. Auntie Gina gives Uncle Benny a kiss on the cheek. Sammy, in his red-and-gold varsity letterman jacket with a huge GVHS across the back, plows into the kitchen. The fridge and cupboard doors slam open and closed. He plays football, has already been scouted for college, and is *always* hungry.

My grandparents' house is my cousins' second home, and I wonder how much they'll hang out here since it's only me and Dad for now. It does feel a little strange without Lolo and Lola, even though it still looks like an old Filipino person's house with the remote control covered in plastic and a giant bamboo fork and spoon hanging on the dining room wall. When they get back from their trip, Dad and I will find our own place somewhere nearby so we can all stay close.

Sammy walks in eating leftovers from a glass container.

"Don't even think about filling up, we're about to eat!" Auntie says, and he marches back into the kitchen. Auntie's tiny compared to her sons, but they always listen to her.

When Sammy comes back out he pulls me into a head-lock and says in a baby voice: "How was your first day of middle school, you sweet wittle boy?" He gives me a noogie, then tries to give me a wet willy, and I crack up.

"How was *your hair's* first day?" I say. Sammy puts all kinds of goop in his spiky do to make it stick straight up—he thinks that impresses girls. One time, Nick replaced Sammy's hair gel with my slime and he got so mad.

"Dinner!" Auntie says, and everyone takes seats, opens pizza boxes, and passes around a bowl of Caesar salad.

"It's my no-carbs week, Mom," Sammy says. "I'm training."

"Live a little, my love, okay?" Auntie smiles at him and it's the permission he needs to pile like a thousand slices onto his plate.

"How's everyone's first week so far, crew?" Dad asks. My cousins launch into their sports lives and Dad's grin practically sparkles. "Still can't believe you made varsity soccer, Nick."

"Couldn't have done it without your extra coaching, Uncle," Nick says.

Dad's missed my school events but never their sports ones. We used to make the two-hour drive every weekend just to watch Nick's soccer matches. I like cheering for my cousins and watching them play, but sometimes it made me jealous.

"Well, you know that's the main reason we wanted your uncle and Alex to move back—free coaching, right?" Uncle Benny laughs.

And now Dad and Uncle Benny and my cousins can't stop—it's like a bottle of shaken seltzer was unscrewed, because everything sports and high school gushes out. Dad in his frozen grin asks so many questions.

I help myself to more salad.

"How about you, Alex?" says Uncle Benny. "What sports are you planning on this year? I remember your cousins tried everything when they were your age."

I pause while I figure out what to say.

"He's thinking about soccer," says Dad.

I shake my head. "I don't know yet . . ."

"Convince him, everyone. Alex would have fun," Dad says, still cheerful from talking with Nick. He says that, but he just wants another trophy for the Shrine. Does he even care about what I want?

I straighten in my chair. "Dad . . . I was thinking about it and . . . I'm not really sure if that's my sport . . ."

"Then what is?" he asks.

"Sliming!" I say, and my cousins both laugh. Hard. I didn't mean to say that, it just flew out. "I mean, it's not a

sport . . . but it's something to keep me busy after school."
Even Dad and Auntie and Uncle have little smiles on their
faces. They're not taking me seriously.

I try to eat my pizza and not look at any of them, but I
feel so silly now. *Don't cry,* I tell myself.

"Alex, buddy, we've talked about this. Sliming's fine, but
let's find other activities you can go deeper into. Something
to help you start sixth grade off with a bang!"

What he means is something to make him proud. Something to brag about like with Nick and Sammy. Something
more his style . . . not mine.

"I'm good at making things." I pick off a pepperoni and
don't look up. I wish I could fling it at him.

"You should totally play soccer," Sammy says. "It'll make
you stronger."

"Yeah, then you can finally beat this guy at arm wres-
tling." Uncle Benny smiles kindly and points to Sammy.

"Never gonna happen," Sammy says. He and Uncle are
trying to lighten things up, but it's not funny to me.

"Ah, leave him alone," Nick says. "Maybe Alex doesn't
need to play anything. He'll be like a cool inventor mogul or
something." Nick nudges my side. "He'll buy me a Lambo
with his first bazillion."

"Alex is good at a lot of things when he puts his mind to
it," Dad says. "We all have a sport we love, right, guys?"

Do they have to talk about me like I'm not sitting
right there?

"Who wants another slice?" Auntie asks. She flashes me a caring smile—she's good at what she calls the distraction method. She always knows when I need the subject changed.

Sammy and Nick raise their plates and Uncle Benny loads them up.

"I can't believe you're both finally here, finally home," Auntie adds. For the rest of the meal Dad doesn't give me his disappointed death stare. He doesn't look at me at all.

WHAT'S SO WRONG WITH MAKING SLIME?

Auntie asks my cousins and me to clean up. We clear the table, wipe it down, and load the dishwasher. Having a store with a takeout bar and a little café has taught us how to do this—for as long as I can remember, Lola and Lolo have always made us help.

Sammy opens the pizza box and spots a couple of stray slices; Auntie playfully slaps his hand when he tries to eat one.

"Why don't you wrap it up and put it in the fridge, sweets?"

"Aye, aye, sir," he says with a stiff salute.

The grown-ups stay at the table. Nick finishes loading the dishwasher and presses Start until it gurgles.

"One more round of hoops?" Nick says.

"Sure," Sammy says. "B-ball, little cuz?" he says to me.

"I don't really feel like it right now." I stuff my hands into my jeans and lean against the counter.

"You still thinking about that weird soccer thing with your dad?" Nick says.

"What's so wrong with making slime?" I ask.

"Uncle just wants you to think about your future," Nick says.

"I'm in sixth grade!" This makes Sammy crack up.

"Yeah, dummy." Sammy lightly smacks Nick's head. "Uncle's probably still mad about that time at Christmas you got red-and-green slime stuck all over Lola's cream-colored couch." They both crack up now. Sammy drapes his arm around me. "Listen, cuz, a little word of advice. If you want the girls at school to like you, maybe choose something cooler than slime. It's . . . kinda gross." He starts laughing.

Nick rolls his eyes. "Don't pay any attention to this fool," he says, pointing to his brother. "And try not to let your dad get to you so much. He's exactly like my dad. And Mom says Lolo was like that, too. It's annoying, but it's how they are." Nick shrugs and he and Sammy head out.

The kitchen door slams behind them, and I can hear Dad and Auntie and Uncle talking from the other room.

"Don't look at me like that," Dad says.

"Let Alex find his own way," Auntie tells him.

"He will, John, Alex is a really good kid," says Uncle Benny. "Kids need to figure things out, too."

"Remember how Anna always wanted a daughter to dress up or go to ballet class with?" Dad says.

Anna. My mom.

"She bought a whole load of tutus before she found out she was pregnant," Auntie says, laughing.

"I used to joke with her that what I really wanted was a son. Somehow I thought it'd be easier than this," Dad says. He laughs at first, but it turns into a sigh. I picture him rubbing his face the way he does whenever something's bothering him. "Alex is a *great* kid, I just wish he'd apply himself more. Put himself out there, you know? Last week he spent all of his allowance on glue. Glue!"

Auntie chuckles hard. "I'd call that *passion.* He's a dreamer *and* a doer."

"You're absolutely right. I guess I have a lot on my mind, sis. I need to make the store work. I'm putting everything into it—our savings, too. If it doesn't start making some real money again, then our dream was for nothing."

I creep to the door and Auntie catches my eye. I step back.

We're not loaded like kids from my old school—we've always had enough, but Dad's also had money issues because of the side businesses he's tried to launch that never made it. Sounds like he's worried about this one now, too.

Auntie joins me in the kitchen. "You all right, sweetie?"

"Did he really put all our savings into the market?"

She gives my shoulder a quick squeeze. "Your dad knows what he's doing. He's a Manalo, remember?"

"But what happens if the store doesn't work out? If we can't make it successful again?"

"I love that you're asking, because it means you care. Every day you remind me more of your mom, you know that?" She pulls me into a quick side hug. "Your father says the things he does because he loves you. You're his everything."

I try to believe her, but when I peek into the dining room, I see Dad shaking his head, his face in his hands.

ONE MORE THING

Once I'm back in my room, I grab a box and turn it upside down on the bed.

Slime stuff.

It's not my room, really, it's Dad's old bedroom, which my grandparents haven't changed since he was in high school. It's still got a soccer ball bedspread and a shelf full of trophies that didn't fit into the Shrine. I reach up, take them all down, and put them one by one into the empty box.

One trophy has a guy swimming, midstroke. I tried doing swim team once, the only sport I sort of liked. During meets I had a strategy: sometimes swim slow, sometimes swim fast. I was determined to win every place so I'd get every color ribbon. A rainbow of them.

"You're such a strong swimmer, Alex. I don't understand why it takes you forever for one lap but other times you're so quick. We should work on your consistency," Dad said, and I told him my goal of winning all the colors. His forehead scrunched up like a raisin. "Why wouldn't you want to just go for first?"

"I do. Just not every single time," I said. He gave me the oddest look.

I never got blue for first, but I won all the other shades.

Winning doesn't have to look like a shiny trophy or a fancy ribbon the way Dad thinks it should—and I'll prove it to him. If there's one thing I know he respects as much as a sports guy, it's a business guy. Maybe slime is the way I can finally impress him.

Dad's old trophies fit neatly into the box like puzzle pieces. I close the lid, shove the box into the deepest corner of my closet, and fill the shelf with bottles of contact lens solution, cans of shaving cream, colorful bottles of shampoo with different yummy scents, permanent markers, rolls of tape, teeny vials of food coloring, a jug of thick glue, and palm-sized plastic containers for my final creations. I bought all of it at the dollar store with birthday money and allowance from doing chores. If Dad doesn't like me using allowance for slime, I'll make my own money from the Slime War.

I step back, dust off my hands, and admire my newly stocked creation station.

I'm going to show Dad—and my whole family—just how cool sliming can be. I'll make my operation work and turn it into its own legend—something Dad can boast about. And if he's spending our savings on the market, this could help. He won't have to feel so worried about money, at least not when it comes to me, because I'll make my own.

One more thing.

I dash downstairs. It's only Dad now, sunk into the couch, clicking away on his laptop.

"Okay," I say, loudly, and he looks up. "I'll play soccer." He doesn't think I stand out like him or like my cousins, but he'll see. If he wants me to play that badly, I'll try. Soccer *and* slime. I'll show him what I can do.

His eyes widen but then a smile stretches across his face. Before he can say anything, I run back upstairs to get sliming. I'll give Dad the kid he wants—in more ways than one.

PURPLE PEOPLE POPPER

Glugs of glue
Shakes of baking soda
Splashes of baby oil
Dashes of purple food coloring
The teeniest, tiniest stray building-block pieces
from an old toy set, to give some texture

The perfect cool and crisp early-morning breeze pours into my room through the open window. I can hear Dad humming downstairs, back from his run.

Every day, Dad's alarm blares at five a.m. sharp. I don't really care, especially not today because it dragged me up and I've got big plans before school starts. In Kidpreneur they taught us that mornings are when your brain's at its best. Dad also liked hearing about how early risers get better grades because they have more focus. But I like mornings because even if I had a miserable day before, I can always start again.

I pull down all the ingredients from my shelf.

Let's.

Get.

Sliming.

I'm going to try something I've seen online—creating without exact measurements. Inventing. Playing. Getting my warm thinking fuzzies going.

Lola has shown me how to cook Filipino dishes like pancit noodles and chicken adobo, but also her favorites that have nothing to do with her homeland, like eggplant parmesan and beef bulgogi, or golden beet salad with walnuts and goat cheese, which I thought sounded gross until I tried it. I'd watch her throw in dashes of this and that, chopping veggies quick as a machine before tossing and stirring and cooking until the whole house smelled wonderful. Whenever she wants me to try a new dish but I don't want to, she reminds me how I ended up liking beets.

Making slime's not the same as cooking, even though I've made edible batches by heating milk and cornstarch and adding fruit flavoring. Tasted just like candy. Still, sometimes I try to guess what ingredients work together.

I squeeze purple shimmery glue into my solution and mix everything with my hand. It's not congealing like it should and runs right through my fingers.

Not great.

I try again with a recipe, and the next batch feels better, smooth and glossy. As I fold and squish, the slime snaps and pops. Nice. I'd spend money on this.

Off to sell.

PIECE. OF. CAKE.

Slime War, day one.

At school I'm in the thick crowd and spot Logan at the lockers. I weave my way through the sea of kids and march up to him.

Logan stuffs in a book and slams the door. When he turns he's wearing a name tag: csc.

"What's that?" I ask.

"Me! Your new chief slime controller!" he says, and I laugh. "Before we team up, let's figure this out. You make the slime, I help you sell it. Sixty-forty." When he says "sixty" he points to himself, and with "forty" he points to me.

I shake my head. "No way. What happened to fifty-fifty?"

"I'm the one with all the connections, Alex. You couldn't do this without me."

Kendra walks up to us and I take a brave little breath—that's what Auntie Gina calls them. I'm not good at talking to girls. Last year one had a crush on me, at least that's what everyone said. Libby Chen followed me everywhere. When

Raj and I would see her, we'd run in the opposite direction as fast as we could.

"Here ya go, Kendra. Fresh batch." I toss her the container.

"You're prompt." She unpops the lid, and I can tell she notices the secret right away because she brings her nose closer for a deep whiff. I added something special—a few drops of essential oil gives it a delicious smell. "Grape? Awesome!" She grins and holds it up to Logan's nose and he sniffs and pokes at it.

"Super bouncy," Logan says, and they laugh.

"Stop! Hurry!" Kendra says under her breath. Their faces turn stony. Kendra quickly puts her hands behind her back, and Logan stiffens next to her. I'm not sure what they're doing until I see a teacher walking by.

The teacher looks at Kendra and Logan, who smile politely.

As soon as he's out of sight, they both let out a breath.

"Wow, that was close," Kendra says.

"Too close," says Logan.

"Who was that?" I ask.

"Mr. Schlansky," Kendra says. "He *hates* slime."

"Anyway, see?" Logan says to Kendra. He nods my way. "I told you he's good."

"I'm your newest fan, Alex." She grins at me and my cheeks get warm.

Everyone has their own way of liking slime. For some

kids it's the satisfying feel, for others it's a happy color or sparkle. I'll have to start figuring out my customers to make things really take off.

"We good?" I ask, and Kendra nods.

Logan punches a fist into the air. "Victory will be ours!" *Piece. Of. Cake.*

I can picture us winning. I can see every kid wanting to sit with us at lunchtime.

"Fifty-fifty," I say, "and that's *my* final offer. *And* you get to keep your CSC title."

"Cool, cool," Logan says. "Just wanted to see what you had in you. Let's strategize. Meet me in the courtyard at lunch—I've got some ideas."

I like idea people. They imagine anything out of nothing and turn it into *something*. Something *real*.

He extends a fist and we bump.

The bell rings and kids stream past us from every direction, including Trevor.

"Hey, Trev," Logan says to him, but Trevor doesn't stop or say anything back. Logan's smile disappears. Logan said they were best friends, but it doesn't seem that way.

As I walk to class a few kids turn toward me and give me sly smiles. The Slime War is on. We're off to a good start.

STARTS WITH A WHISPER

In science class, Mrs. Graham greets everyone at the door. "Good morning, Alex," she says with a smile.

I settle into my seat and Logan whispers across the rows, "Lunchtime we kill it."

Last night I made batches of all my best slime, but I didn't have time to think much about the selling part. I'm glad Logan's on my side.

"How? Where?" I whisper.

"Haven't made a final decision yet, but wherever we end up, we keep moving until it's over. We can't let any teachers get suspicious."

"Should we put up signs or something?" I ask.

He looks at me like I've got ten eyeballs and twelve nostrils. "I just said not suspicious! You want to get caught before we even start?"

Oh, right.

Before I have a chance to whisper back, Mrs. Graham

eyes us and makes her time-to-quiet-down peace sign, so that's the end of that.

It's hard to pay attention when I have slime on my mind—how we'll sell and how we'll win. Then, midway through our lesson is when I see it.

It starts with a whisper.

A chain reaction.

Logan looks around, and when Mrs. Graham turns her back he leans toward the girl in front of him and says something into her ear. Then she does the same thing to the kid in front of her, and up and up and sideways and over and all around the class those whispers travel, from desk to desk, kid to kid.

All day until lunchtime it keeps happening.

Notes passed.

Cupped hands by ears.

Strangers giving me a knowing nod. Every sixth grader is shooting glances my way, but I don't know who they are yet.

The bell rings and I grab my backpack full of loot. It's slime time.

CUSTOMERS!

I make it through the next few periods, but the whole time my stomach's doing loopy roller coasters. At lunch Logan meets me at the lockers.

"Ready?" I ask.

"One important thing we have to do first," he says with seriousness. "We need a secret handshake."

I laugh, but then I think about it. Handshakes are the ultimate body language. In Kidpreneur we learned the importance of a good handshake. It means:

- You're confident.
- You're making a promise.
- You're setting something in motion.
- You know what you're doing.

And you have to give a firm one, not a wet-fish one with a floppy wrist.

"You're absolutely right," I say.

Instead of a formal grasp and a shake, shake, shake, we want to make ours special. We try a few moves—slapping palms and bumping knuckles, things like that—but it's awkward and we crack up.

"Oooh, I know," Logan says. He demonstrates a high five and two quick fist bumps.

"Not bad, but how about an oomph at the end?" I add exploding fingers.

"One more." He adds a pullback.

We try the whole thing again as fast as we can: high five, two fist bumps, exploding fingers, pullback. Hey, not bad!

"Done!" I say. "Let's get selling."

Logan recruited his friends Carl and Pepper to help us with the Slime War—Carl as publicity magician and Pepper as senior VP of goo relations. They'll bring a lot to our team.

My head spins with strategy questions, but I don't have time to think about it because Carl spots us and drags me by the arm into position: at the very farthest table, adjacent to the courtyard, tucked behind a tree.

The courtyard blares with commotion, only we're not in the thick of it.

I plonk down my backpack and the slime containers rattle.

"Shouldn't we be more . . . find-able?" I ask.

"Nah, we're good," Logan says.

"But there's no foot traffic here." I expected at least a couple of buyers to show up after that whole whisper show earlier, but we're the only ones waiting.

"People are still eating. Patience!" Logan throws up his hands.

He's right. If we slime, they will come . . . except after what feels like forever, we still don't have any customers.

"We should move into the courtyard now," I suggest. "We can put some samples out and start figuring out who our consumer base is." Maybe throwing in some fancy Kidpreneur stuff will help them take me seriously.

"Good idea." Pepper nods.

Carl asks, "What's a consumer base?"

"Just a fancy way of saying the people who buy your product," I say. "And hopefully they'll keep buying it."

"Well, once we *have* a consumer base, I don't think we should sell out in the open like that with everyone watching. What if there are teachers there?" Carl says. "We chose this secret spot to be strategic."

I can't take this anymore. "I'm going to tell people where they can find us."

Carl digs a pack of cards out of his lunch bag, shuffles, and fans them out in front of Logan's face. "If I can guess the card Logan pulls out, we change spots."

Logan bites into his hamwich and waves the cards away.

"We shouldn't copy Meadow. Don't worry, Alex, people will discover us here," he mumbles with a full mouth.

Carl throws the cards onto the table. "Look!" He straightens and elbows me in the side as two kids march our way.

Slimers! Yes!

I pull out my best containers and line them up—but they pass us right by.

Carl shrugs. "If we fail with the slime, we can always sell merch and swag."

"No, we can't." Pepper throws her hands in the air and says, "What about the rules?"

Another kid steps up to the table, and Carl elbows me again and we both straighten up. I flash my best salesman smile.

Okay. For real now.

Logan gets up, smooths down his hair, and clears his throat. The boy comes to our table and picks up a container of Toxic Waste Tornado. "Nice choice, our bestseller," Logan says. "You won't regret making it your first purchase with us."

The kid shakes the little tub but throws it back onto the table. "Won't regret booger slime? Just had to see it for myself." He laughs and walks away.

"What was *that* all about?" Logan asks.

"Wait here, boys," Pepper says, and she jets off, her red beanie getting smaller as she runs farther away.

"Okay. What was I saying? Consumer base." I pull a notebook from my backpack. "Let's make a list of the different kinds of slime I made, and we'll keep track of who buys what based on their demographics," I say, and Carl and Logan give me funny looks.

From a distance, we see Pepper's red beanie again. She sprints toward us, out of breath. "Look at all these people buying Meadow's slime!" She holds up her phone and zooms in on a picture of Meadow, Kristina B., and their entourage out in the courtyard, a long, snaking line of buyers.

"And how's *that* not going to get everyone caught?" I say. "They're playing with fire!"

Logan grabs the phone for a closer look. "I know what she's doing. They've got books out like they're studying, but it's all a front. When teachers see it—and Goody Two-shoes kiss-up Meadow and her minions—they won't suspect anything." He shakes his head.

"Meadow and Her Minions sounds like a good band name," Carl says.

"Why didn't we come up with that tactic?" I say. "We're going to have to catch up big-time. We can still claim a table out there." I get up to leave, but Pepper stops me.

"Wait, that's not all," she says. "Meadow's squad is playing *dirty.*"

"What do you mean?" says Logan.

"At least ten people told me that she told them your slime's contaminated!"

"My products are pure and pristine, nothing wrong with them!" I say.

"Yeah, but they believe her. Look." Pepper plays a video on her phone. There's catchy music and hands making slime, exactly like every how-to I've ever watched. Totally unoriginal.

White blocky words flash on and off:

Alex's secret slime recipe:

Glue

Smidgen of snot

Hairy butt-scent

As these words pop up, so do sound effects of *spurt*s and *splat*s and *fart*s.

"She made a mean meme and butt-burped it!" Logan says, and he and Carl can't stop laughing. "Well played, Meadow, well played." I swat Logan on the shoulder.

The video ends in applause with Meadow's face coming into focus and her evil, gravelly voice: "You want that? Or you want this?"

A giant glob of gooey, glorious slime—the smoothest, prettiest batch you've ever seen: "Try some of Meadow's Miraculous Miracle. It's oozy, gooey, stretchy, authentic— and organic, with no GMOs . . ." Her face fills the screen with an intense expression: "And no boogers."

*Oooh*s and *aaah*s and applause blare from an audio track.

"Buy *my* slime," Meadow says, walking around a table of popular-looking kids.

Then, the final image: a container of slime labeled ALEX'S SAD SLIME with an animated crying emoji.

Carl shakes his head. "Can't believe she'd stoop so low."

"Yeah, but she put a lot of work into it," Logan says. "I'm kind of impressed."

Pepper shrugs. "They don't call her Meadow Mac*Fear*son for nothing."

How can they be so calm when my name and *my* hard work were just ruined?

I scan the space around us. Zero customers.

Someone taps me on the shoulder—Kendra. Whew. Back for more. This'll get things going.

"Our number one customer. What do you want to try next?" I ask. "Five-Way Floam? Poisoned Peach? Sitting on a Cloud?"

Kendra frowns. "A full refund."

"What? Why?" Pepper says.

Kendra slaps something hard onto the table. "It dried up!"

"No way, I—" I start to say, but Logan grabs it and throws it to the ground, where it skips and rolls like a rock.

Shoot. I must have mixed the wrong ratio or something.

"Do you want to try a different batch?" asks Carl. "We have sooo much. A ton. A whole bag full—"

"She gets the point," I say.

Kendra shakes her head and keeps her palm out. Logan fishes crumpled bills from his pocket and places them on her hand.

"You should stick to magic," Kendra says to him, and she skips off.

I turn to Logan. "What just happened?"

"We're doomed," Carl says. "That's what."

"No worries, people! It's only day one," Pepper says.

"Dude, just burn Meadow back. Make your own video starring Meadow MacFartson," says a boy with red hair and freckles as he walks by with a few other kids. They snicker.

"Do it, Alex. The burn video," another kid says. They keep laughing and nod in agreement.

I shake my head. "Sorry. I don't slime that way." I notice a few kids at a table nearby watching us really closely. A girl with a bun on each side of her head nods like she's agreeing with me.

Pepper rolls her eyes at the redheaded kid. "Go away, Rudy." She turns her back to him. Logan and Rudy look at each other for a second before Rudy and his friends walk off.

"We'll have to restrategize, that's all," Logan says to me.

The bell rings and I sling my backpack on, heavy with what we haven't sold.

TOO LATE

Slime War, day one, full failure. And now I get to play soccer. *Yippee!*

Dad bounds down the stairs whistling and skipping two steps at a time. When he jumps off the final step, he shoots his arms up like a gymnast. "What do you give me on a scale of ten?"

What dad does this?

"Zero point five—for effort," I say, and we crack up.

"Ready for our first practice?" he asks.

I close my eyes and imagine doing something I've never managed to do: kick a ball into a goal.

It's something I learned from Sammy whenever he wants to win a football game. If you picture the thing you want to come true, it will happen. Except now I've kept my eyes closed for too long because in my daydream, suddenly a ball whacks me in the head and people in the stands point and laugh.

"How good are the other kids?" I ask.

I thought I could show Dad what I'm made of, but I'm not sure anymore—and now it's too late. Dad's still whistling and bouncing around.

I grab the bag Auntie brought over last night of Nick's soccer gear from when he was my age. Dad wanted me to use his stuff that he dug out, but it was too worn.

I sit on the couch and slip on a pair of Nick's old but clean soccer socks, rolling them up and over my knees, and step into his old cleats. His stuff's almost like new because Auntie said he outgrew everything so quickly. I'm pretty sure I'd have to drink a million protein shakes and do ten thousand strength-training burpees to get as tall and strong as my cousins.

The unfair thing about middle school is the way scrawny sixth graders like me are mixed in with kids who've already got six-packs and beards and voices as deep as Darth Vader's. When I see pictures of Nick and Sammy, they didn't look as small as I do now. Or at least as small as I feel sometimes.

Dad's not super tall, but he always says his height didn't affect his agility. And Mom wanted to be a professional dancer, but people said she was too short. It made her sad until she read about a tall dancer in the eighteenth century who was so popular, that's the only reason why people these days think dancers need to be tall.

Last but not least, I pull out a neon cloth headband and smoosh it onto my head.

"What's that?" Dad asks.

I point to the bag. "Nick gave it to me. He said it'd help me keep my hair out of my face when I'm running."

Dad eyes it for a moment and says, "It's kind of like what the girls wear, right?"

"Plenty of players wear these." Why's he asking? He *knows* this.

"Fair enough, but I still think you need a haircut."

He doesn't think boys should have long hair. *Who cares,* I want to say, but I nod. I'm nervous enough as it is.

"Okay, it's soccer time!" He slings a big mesh bag full of fluorescent yellow-and-orange soccer balls over his shoulder and we head out. I try to picture what I want: me as an awesome soccer player—I'll even take not-so-bad!—but when I close my eyes all I see is failing, and suddenly all I want is out.

G-BEATZ

In front of Golden Valley Middle School there's a field of turf so new and so bright green that it seems like something too perfect to play on. We pull into the parking lot. Dad turns off the ignition and pauses a second to look me in the eye. "I'm glad you're trying this, Alex." I clasp my hands in my lap and try to smile back, but my head's buzzing and my stomach's playing its own match right now. I grab the mesh bag.

We walk onto the field, where a few parents wait with their kids. Some boys are already jogging around or stretching. I'm about to play with kids who've probably done this their whole lives. My heart jumps.

A man approaches Dad with a hearty handshake. "John! I'd heard the rumor you moved back, but I had to see for myself! Nice to see you!"

Other parents come over and chime in with their greetings, and Dad beams.

At a goalpost I set down the bag. A couple of boys kick a ball back and forth and look up at me.

"Hey, it's Slime Boy," says one of them. Trevor. He laughs. "I'm just messin' with ya. Guess what? Our dads used to be buddies." Trevor nods toward the guy who said hi when we first got here—he and Dad are still chatting. "He said we might even win this season if your dad's coaching. He bets you're just as good."

I guess I'll let him believe it as long as I can.

The parents leave and Dad sprints over. We huddle up in the center.

"Okay, men, before we go out there, we need to figure out our team name for good luck. Let's hear everyone's sug- gestions. Then we'll put it to a vote."

Whenever Dad shoots hoops with my cousins he calls them men, too.

We glance around at each other and start shouting:

"The Lasers!"

"The Farta-lonas!"

"The Benchwarmers!"

"The Look Ma, No Hands!"

Dad nods at each player, going around the circle to give everyone a chance, until he gets to me. He looks at me. Then everyone else does, too.

Think, Alex. It's hard to do that under pressure.

"Umm . . . the . . . Golden . . . Beets?" I say.

Every boy shoots me the weirdest look.

"The *Organic* Golden Beets?" I add. I have no idea why. It's the first thing that popped into my brain.

"You mean like the *vegetable*?" asks Trevor, and he snickers.

"Beets improve athletic performance," I say. "And they're packed with nutrients, so they'll help us play better."

"It doesn't mean we have to call ourselves after some gross vegetable," Rudy says, and pretends to barf.

A boy next to me raises his hand.

"Yes? Jacob?" Dad says.

"Well . . . it could work . . . if it's like a beat. You know, like in music," Jacob says.

"How about the Beats but with a *Z*?" says another kid.

"And *G* for *golden* because we're going to win gold," says one boy. "So, like, the Organic G-Beatz."

"That's a really good hip-hop name," chimes in another kid.

"Yeah, and our catchphrase can be *We're gonna Beatz ya!*" says another boy. We all start laughing, except for Rudy and Trevor, who roll their eyes. Somehow everyone's nodding and agreeing with my suggestion. Trevor looks around and suddenly he joins in, too, laughing loudly.

"The Organic G-Beatz?" Dad says. I feel myself wanting to smile, but I can tell Dad's not into it. "When my team won championships we were the Razors. Now *there's* a star soccer team name—quick, easy to remember, descriptive," he says, but my beet comment for some reason has gotten everyone excited. The best ideas start with the barest glint of something, and everyone gives their input until it shines.

Trevor says, "Who votes for the G-Beatz?" and most hands raise.

Dad shakes his head and chuckles. "Okay then, the Organic G-Beatz it is. How about the G-Beatz for short? And maybe it's a smart move, having a stealth name. They'll never expect us to swoop in and win every single time."

At least I helped with the team name. Maybe I won't bomb so bad after all.

SCORE!

For the next two hours we warm up, then practice our skills: sprints, drills, passes. This part's not that hard. I can kind of fake it, but we haven't played a real game yet.

"Scrimmage time!" Dad shouts, and he splits us up into two groups. He throws orange jersey tank tops to my group and we yank them over our shirts—the other group stays in their regular shirts—and he begins to randomly assign positions. "Everyone will have the chance to play every position at some point." He looks at me. "Alex, take midfield. Offense."

Dad just got done telling us that offensive midfielders are quick, fast, and strong. They attack.

Why's he doing this to me?

I bite my lip and walk over to the spot, wishing hard that the ball doesn't come my way.

We start.

I run a lot and am keeping up with the other players. But then the ball flies my way and I shield my head and duck.

Some of the kids laugh, others frown at me. I hate this stupid game.

"Eyes on the ball, everyone!" Dad shouts.

The ball crisscrosses the field and the other kids kick with such confidence. One boy punts it hard and it comes hurtling toward me. I flinch and block my face by instinct, and it flies right past me to another player.

I look over at Dad and he's frowning.

The ball gets kicked down the field. Another boy boots it—I wince and shield myself again—but it lands in front of my feet with no one right by to guard it.

What luck! This is my chance.

I kick and move forward with the ball, keeping my eyes ahead like we practiced. The goalpost comes into view and I kick the ball in as hard as I can.

It hits the net.

Score!

"What are you doing?" a kid yells, and I notice Trevor clutching his sides, laughing hysterically.

Dad's waving his arms and shouting: "Other direction, Alex!"

"Wrong goal," says Trevor, who's been looking strong and confident all practice.

The whole team laughs, so hard, like they're all in on the best joke. I'm sweating from running and kicking and my hair sticks to my neck. I feel like I'm the only one panting.

"Have you never played soccer before?" a boy asks.

"Newb!" yells Rudy, and he busts up. I'm too embarrassed to respond or look at Dad, or anyone.

I have played, in fourth grade, but I kept crying before practice because I didn't want to, and I remember the hugest relief when Dad let me stop. Except he said: *One day we'll try again.*

Dad blows his whistle. "Practice is over! Huddle up one last time, team! Good going, everyone!"

He can't mean me, too. I stare down at my cleats.

Dad gives a little pep talk, then says, "On three . . . G-Beatz!" We all give a hands-in and the rest of the boys shout.

Finally we're done. I help Dad pack up, but his smile from earlier is gone. We walk to the car. "What happened to all those times we kicked a ball around, Alexander? Did you forget everything I taught you?" I yank my shin guards out of my socks and look away. What do I even say to that? He looks at me like he feels bad now. "You did fine."

I slip the headband off—it's soaked with sweat. "Yeah," I say, but I still don't meet his gaze.

"Listen, whenever I'm scared of something, son, I do it anyway. It helps."

"I'll try again next practice."

"If you're confused about how things work, just ask me, okay?"

"I know, Dad, I got it."

"Excellent." He nods.

Trevor's dad catches up to us. "Looks like your shooter could use some work," he says to Dad with a little laugh.

"He'll get there," Dad says quietly, because I think he doesn't want me to hear, but it's just loud enough.

YOU KNOW WHAT TO DO

Slime War, day two.

When Logan and I walk into first-period science, Meadow's already there kissing up to Mrs. Graham with her fake smile. Meadow pulls a bouquet of flowers in a glass vase out of a brown paper bag. Mrs. Graham says some gushy *Thank yous* and *Oh, you and your mother didn't have to do that!*

"Of course we did! You're my favorite teacher of all time!" Meadow's smile is so stretched it might freeze that way. Even my most elastic slime would have snapped already.

"What's she doing?" I whisper to Logan.

"It's fine, she's playing the game. Meadow's sucked up to all our teachers ever since preschool, and we need that to not get us caught. It keeps the teachers happy and not suspicious," Logan says. "Her mom owns a flower shop, and Meadow won't ever shut up about how they're so successful because they do every wedding and bar mitzvah in town."

The bell rings and our class quiets. "Before we launch in this morning, I'm changing our seating chart," says Mrs. Graham.

She has us all stand to one side of the room while she goes to each desk station and calls out two names. Logan gets paired with someone new, and so do the rest of the kids. She reads names two by two, and I'm left standing until the last desk and the last two students.

"Alex and Meadow, you know what to do." She points to the station behind Logan's.

Great.

"Please read the worksheet while I set up the video," Mrs. Graham says as she busies herself at the large projection screen in the front of the room. We start to read.

Logan catches my attention and nods toward the kid sitting next to him.

"Customer," he mouths.

"Not now," I mouth back.

I look from Mrs. Graham's back to Logan mouthing "Win, win, win!" to my competition seated next to me, engrossed in her worksheet and scooting in her chair as far away from me as she can like I'm about to give her cooties.

Well, it's only one little tub.

I slip the container from my backpack and am sliding it to the corner of the table for Logan to grab, when Mrs. Graham turns around. Her eyes zero right in on the slime. She marches over.

"What is this?" she asks.

My breathing feels hurried. "I . . . uh—"

"Sorry, Mrs. Graham," Meadow says. "That's—that's *my* slime." The whole class stays silent. "I took it out of my backpack to get to my binder. I know we're not supposed to have it here, and it will never ever happen again." Meadow doesn't look at me as she says any of this.

Mrs. Graham shakes her head. "Meadow, of all people. You know the rules." Our teacher extends her palm and Meadow plonks my slime onto it. "You've never gotten a warning before, so consider this it."

All the prying eyes turn back around and our class settles into their work again. Meadow writes something on the corner of her notebook and points it at me with her pencil:

You're welcome.

My eyes get wide. Did *Meadow* just save me?

After class, Logan's by my side and we head into the crowded hallway.

"You almost got me caught," I say.

"Yeah, that was close. Sorry. But next time you'll know not to pay any attention to me." He smiles, and I can only laugh.

"Why'd Meadow take the blame? Strange, huh?"

Logan shrugs. "If I know Meadow, she's probably cooking something up."

Trevor and his group walk by doing their thing, laughing so hard like sixth grade's so easy for them.

"Hey, Trev!" Logan says, but the boys keep going. Logan stays quiet, and I feel kind of bad for him. We keep walking down the hall.

"Why'd you want to be in the Slime War?" I ask. I don't know a lot about Logan yet. I wonder if he needs the money, too.

"If I tell you something, will you swear not to ever say anything?"

I cross my heart.

"Trev always wanted to be cooler, and now that he's friends with Rudy . . ." He shakes his head like he's embarrassed. "Maybe if we win the Slime War, I'll get my friend back. Is that dumb?"

"Nope. Not at all," I say. I didn't have close buddies at my old school besides Raj. It would have been really lonely without him.

"What about you?" Logan asks.

I tell him how I want to help my dad with money. "And the whole being the heroes of the school thing still sounds pretty awesome." I nod. "My dad wants a superstar for a kid." Logan listens closely, the way a friend might, while I share what happened at practice.

His eyes turn determined. "Then let's win. Meet back at lunch."

GOOD INVESTMENT

At the lockers, Carl and Pepper are waving their arms frantically. As I get closer, a bunch of kids crowd around us.

"I'll take one of the Birthday Cake Confettis," says a girl to Pepper.

"Two for me," another says to Carl. "Make that one Birthday Cake and one Oozy Eyeball."

"What's going on?" I ask.

"We're open for business," says Logan.

There are so many hands exchanging money and slime, I can't keep track of who's who.

I turn to my CSC: a high five, two quick fist bumps, exploding fingers, pullback.

"Where'd all these buyers come from?" I ask.

"Him." Logan nods toward a boy who walks past. We make eye contact briefly. He's a tall, older-looking kid—the handsome kind who'd star in a teen vampire show.

The guy plays with an amazing batch I made—the

Gooriffic—a mix of sleek colors and smooth textures that feels like silk (I added in generous dollops of soft, sweet-smelling lotion). He tosses it from hand to hand as he saunters by, and girls near my locker give him swoony giggles.

"Who's *that*? He didn't buy any slime from us. Did he?" I say.

"Nope," says Logan. "Because *we* paid *him*." Logan points to himself and Carl.

"We bribed him?"

"Paid, bribed . . . whatever! He's an influencer. We need him on our side."

"A what?"

"People who look so cool that everyone wants what they have," Carl says. "He posted your slime online, but not in a mean Meadow kind of way—more in a come-get-your-own-and-be-so-suave-and-perfect-like-me-the-eighth-grader way. He's *that* respected. And he has a ton of followers. It's marketing. It's my job!"

"Yeah . . . but how much did you pay him?"

"Thirty bucks."

"I don't have thirty bucks!"

"It's fine, I used my lawn-mowing money. We've already made it back," Carl says.

I ponder this and he's right. "ROI. Good thinking. Good investment," I say.

"R-O-what?" Logan says.

"Return on investment. It means you make back what you spent—plus more," Pepper says, and I nod.

"But are you sure this isn't going against the rules?" I ask.

"Nothing in the rules that says we can't invest in our own marketing. Meadow chose a smear campaign. Ours is ten times more sophisticated." Carl taps his head. "Trust me."

The bell rings, but no one's rushing off to class. Kids are still swarming us.

"People are loving your slime, Alex!" says Pepper. "Only one person has wanted an exchange since it was drying out."

"Those are good odds," I say. The demand's high—another good sign. Except we can't keep up with supply if we keep going strong like this. It gives me an idea.

"I should have enough slime to get us through the rest of this week, but you guys want to come over this weekend and we'll make some more? I could use help with our inventory, then we can sell the final batches on Monday. We can fix the drying-out problem, too."

Logan's brow wrinkles. "Like I said before, I'm not much of a maker."

When we first took over the market, Dad said he had to work every job there—stocking shelves, cleaning, register— so he could understand the business from every angle. If I show Logan, Carl, and Pepper how to make the slime, they'll feel like it's their business, too, and that will help us rock this war.

"It's just having fun," Pepper says.

"Exactly," I say. "And I'll have everything ready so all you have to do is show up, follow directions, and mix."

Carl and Pepper playfully shake Logan by his shoulders until finally all three say, "We're in."

MY THRONE

We sold every tub of slime in my backpack! Rulers of sixth grade, here we come.

After school I pedal off to the market for Dad's daily dose of chores, and later this afternoon I have soccer again. The G-Beatz have practice every day this week with our first game this weekend, and I'm terrified. Whenever I'm on the field my head feels so jumbled—a little like how the market looks as I walk in, half taken apart with things all around. Auntie hung a banner that says EXCUSE OUR MESS WHILE WE REMODEL!

Somehow I don't mind the chaos as much in here, though. It feels like we're making things happen.

"Hi, Dad," I say.

"How was your day, buddy?" He's painting different shades of white onto a cream wall across from the register.

I want to tell him about my slime business—get him excited, too—but the more I think about it, the more I want to wait until I win the war. Bigger news is better news.

"School was fine."

"Happy to hear it."

I tackle my tasks of packing boxes and bins. Our whole family's pitching in on this remodel, which means cleaning, painting, reorganizing, and designing a new menu for the hot-food bar. We're ordering a new MANALO MARKET sign for the storefront. We're keeping the shelves organized by different parts of Asia, but squishing them a bit because Dad wants to make room for some fancy-schmancy gourmet items that he thinks will bring in new customers.

I close a box of knickknacks, ceramic elephants and Chinese dragons, that Dad doesn't want to carry anymore.

"Why can't we keep selling these?" I ask.

"You know how much dust those things had?"

Dad swipes a few streaks of paint onto the wall. I climb onto the rice sacks, give them a slap, and watch him from up high.

"Isn't plain ol' white plain ol' boring?" I say. Lolo and Lola have a pretty teal wall behind the register where they used to hang framed photos of Dad and Auntie Gina's school sports teams that the store sponsored. Now there are faded squares and the pictures are stacked up in towers on the floor.

"Trying to make it a little more uniform in here," he says.

"Do . . . do Lolo and Lola know what your new plans for the market are?"

"No, they said they wanted to be surprised. They'll be so happy to see this place looking fresh and new."

I catch Dad eyeing the market's first dollar bill. He glances around like he's about to do something illegal, and very gingerly pulls out a metal tack from one corner where it sticks to the wall.

"What are you doing?" I say.

"We'll hang it back up in an even better spot. It'll be great to get some new faces in here, huh? We'll be like the hip new spot on the block."

"It's not hip if you call it hip." And definitely not if he's going to want to sell olive oil and unfinished tree stumps like our neighbors. Dad laughs. "And we've already got a bunch of loyal shoppers," I say, hopping off my rice throne.

"Which is wonderful, but there are tons of potential shoppers around here, especially from the hospital and those big business parks. This place could be a gold mine, but we have to help it get there."

I grab some of the rice-wrapper candies from Lolo's stash and pop one. The wrapper melts on my tongue.

"And you know what," Dad says, "no more giving away free stuff. There are some traditions we don't need to keep."

My eyes get big and I nearly choke. Lolo's going to hate that. Kids always come to our market instead of the giant Asian grocery store nearby because of Lolo's free candy.

Dad ties up some garbage bags, and that's my cue to take them out.

The sun's up high and warms my face. I get a boost on

sunny days. Uncle Benny said that's because our body re-leases a chemical when we're out in sunshine to make us feel happy. Uncle Benny knows a lot of cool things.

In the back of our building there's another parking lot and a long chain-link fence that separates this strip mall from the park near school, with its grassy lawn, picnic tables, and beds of flowers. My cousins and I used to play there a lot. We'd go to the store early on weekends and make so much noise Lola had no choice but to boot us out. We'd hop the fence and spend hours there. But when my cousins got older they stopped doing that with me. I've never told them this, but I miss playing like that. They'd probably think I'm a baby for still wanting to now.

I toss the bags into a giant bin, and through the fence I spot . . . Meadow? I think it's her. I walk closer. She looks around like she's making sure no one's watching, then plucks flowers—fluffy white ones Lola admires, but also some golden poppies—the California state flower! Whoa. If she pulled that move in a state park I'm pretty sure she'd get thrown in the slammer—that's the rumor, anyhow.

I recognize those white flowers, they're what Meadow gave to Mrs. Graham as her suck-up gift. Why would she do that? I thought Logan said her family owned a flower shop.

I head back inside, and Dad's done with painting. The store's first dollar is resting on the counter, like noth-ing special.

"Any other chores you need me to do before I go home?" I ask Dad. I want to do some slime-sperimenting.

Dad looks up from his clipboard. "No, but an old friend's dropping by—going to give me some business advice. He owns a bunch of commercial property around town, including our block. Why don't you stick around for a bit. As a future CEO, I think you'd learn something."

I want to escape out the back door—I need to get home and do more strategizing—but the bell chimes and in walks a friendly-looking guy.

"John! Nice to see you!" says the man, who's older than Dad, though they look similar, like they could be related. I feel that way sometimes when I meet other Filipino people because we know where we came from.

The man and Dad greet each other. "You must be Alex," he says to me.

He introduces himself as Kevin Santiago and extends his hand. I take it—firm grip. A sure sign he's successful. Maybe I will stick around.

SQUEEZE THE DAY

"It's been a while, let me give you a quick tour," Dad says, and they begin walking around, talking nonstop.

"Alex, I've always admired your family's market," Mr. Santiago says. "It's a part of life around here. The only place where my family could find everything they needed."

I've heard this story before. I like knowing that somehow, my family's helped make people feel at home.

"So, Kevin, what's the scoop on the space next door?" Dad asks. "We're so curious to find out who our new neighbors will be."

"Good question. I've been reviewing applicants, and there's a group of young entrepreneurs with an impressive business plan—and the capital to make it happen."

"What kind of business?" I ask.

"Get this. Robot arms." He laughs. "Sounds outrageous, but they're revolutionizing the food service industry— flipping burgers, prepping meals, removing the chance of any human error. They want to do a trial run with a juice bar. Here, I'll show you."

Mr. Santiago pulls out his phone and plays us a video of a robot arm in a glass case in the middle of a huge mall. A kid touches and swipes through commands on a screen in front of the robot station, and a woman flashes her credit card in front of it. Out of nowhere a nice lady's voice says: "Thank you for juicing with us! Squeeze the day!"

The robot arms whir and in Rube Goldberg style, a ramp lined with oranges tilts and the fruit slides down, spins onto a wagon wheel, lops into a squeezer, and the liquid drains into a cup. Another arm scoops in ice—*plop! plop! plop!*—and yet another arm secures the top and presses a button.

A final robot arm pokes in a straw and slides the drink through a tube.

"Voilà! Juice!" Mr. Santiago says. "Wild, huh?"

"Interesting," Dad says, though he doesn't look very impressed.

"What do you think?" Mr. Santiago asks me.

I shrug. "You can't really say hi to a robot."

"Did you know Alex wants to become a business owner, too?" Dad starts telling his friend about my Kidpreneur win. "Maybe one day Alex will want to take over this place."

"You know, I started dreaming up business ideas around the time I was your age, Alex," Mr. Santiago says.

He tells us how he came here as a baby with his family

from the Philippines and his parents worked many jobs to put him through college. As a boy he started with a paper route, chucking rolled-up newspapers into people's yards before the sun came up. As a teen he sold magazine subscriptions around his neighborhood.

"I started from practically nothing. All I had was my imagination."

"You taking notes?" Dad says to me with a smile.

"When I was selling magazines I knocked on every door, and after that I made my parents drive me to other neighborhoods, so I could knock on even more." He chuckles. "I got really good at pitching people."

Door-to-door—that must have taken a lot of time. His sales skyrocketed. And suddenly, inspiration hits.

"Hey, Dad, can I go over to Logan's?"

"Who's Logan?"

"A new . . ." I want to say "friend," but technically we're business partners. "A kid in sixth grade."

"What about your homework?"

"I did it during study hall."

Dad nods and says, "Be back by four for practice."

I run out the door before he can change his mind.

THE CINCHER

I'm thinking about doors as I knock on Logan's. I've run into Logan in the mornings on our way to school, so I know which house is his.

He answers. "I know how we can cinch the Slime War," I say, shifting my backpack, full of slime boxes.

"Yes, but is it as perfect as this magic?" Logan asks. He lifts his arm and out of his sleeve pops a cute little whiskered face sniffing the air.

"Aww, hi, Bubbie," I say, reaching out to rub Logan's pet rat between his soft ears. Logan's told me all about his two pet rats and showed me lots of pictures. One is named Mochi and the other is Bubbie, a chonker with smooth white fur and a dark gray stripe down his back. Logan plops Bubbie onto his shoulder and I have to admit—he's cute.

"Why not just a dog or a cat?" I ask.

"Don't judge! This little guy's potty-trained and loves waffles and makes the best magician's assistant when I pull him out of a hat . . . except for all the horrified screams from the audience." Logan snorts. "Okay, back to your plan. Tell me more."

"There's some private schools around here, right? And a few elementary schools? So that means not all the kids in our neighborhood go to Golden Valley?" I say, and Logan nods. "We should hit up as many families as we can. Let's go door-to-door and sell. We'll have an edge that Meadow hasn't thought of yet."

"Brilliant! Even stuffy uniform kids like to slime. There's nothing in the rules about going off campus. Wait here. I'll put Bubbie back in his pen and get my shoes."

"Hey, you got any bow ties, too?" I yell as he runs into the house. "Maybe we should do this the Melvin Moore way!"

Logan comes running back outside holding up two red bow ties. "They're my dad's from when he sang in a barbershop quartet." He's also carrying a black metal *Star Wars* lunch box that looks vintage but in excellent condition, no dents or scratches. "This is a good-luck charm. Let's use it for all the moolah we're about to rake in."

"I bet if you sold that as a collector's item you'd make even more."

"No way. It was my mom's when she was a kid—it's her favorite movie ever. Mine, too," he says.

"Makes sense." My dad told Mr. Santiago that maybe one day I'd inherit the store. I like the idea of owning something that my dad did that *his* dad did. A special con-nection no one else can have but us, like Logan and his mom have, too.

"Ready to go?" Logan asks.

We clip on our bow ties and run down the block.

BE CHARMING

"**W**hen going door-to-door, use one simple strategy," Logan says. "Be. Charming."

The first house has pebbles instead of a lawn, and spinning pinwheels line the walkway. I can tell these people will want to support neighborhood kids.

Logan reaches to ring the bell, but I block him. "Let's knock. It's more profesh."

We knock, loudly and confidently.

A man answers wearing fuzzy pink pajamas, even though it's the late afternoon. A white cockatoo rests on his head.

"Uh . . . hello," says Logan.

The bird hops down onto the man's shoulder and repeats: "Uh, hello! Uh, hello!"

Logan and I crack up.

"Are you laughing at my Parry?" The man looks to his side. "I'm sure they're not laughing at *you*, Parry."

"Laughing at you! Laughing at you!" the bird shouts.

"No, sir, it's just that . . . we didn't expect to see him. He's sweet, though," I say.

"Would you like to buy some slime?" Logan asks.

"Slime? I'm not into slime," the man says.

"Not into slime! Not into slime!" the bird says.

Logan and I look at each other and bust up again. It's hard to keep a straight face.

"You don't have to be into slime to—" I say, but the door slams.

"Rude," Logan says.

"It's fine. We'll make that our warm-up," I say, and we go to the next house.

When I did Cub Scouts, Dad was troop leader and we had to sell popcorn: butter, caramel, and cheesy (my favorite). One afternoon we waited outside a grocery store, and even though everyone smiled at us, they passed by with their shopping carts and didn't buy a single kernel. Until I made a suggestion: "Let's move over there." I pointed to a gym across the street. Dad loved the idea, and that's when we sold out.

If Logan and I want this to work, we have to keep going.

At the next house a mom in sweatpants holding a crying baby on her hip answers the door. A few more screaming toddlers run around behind her. We give our pitch and she shouts: "I'll take five!"

Our first sale of the day leads to a burst of good luck.

As we go down the block, that one yes snowballs into more yeses until our lunch box fills with dollar bills. We get more sure of ourselves with each house.

"It worked!" We grin, but Logan shifts from one leg to the other.

"What are you doing?"

"I have to go to the bathroom," he says. "I've been holding it . . . I see Carl's house . . . be right back!" He sprints across the street.

"Catch up to me!" I yell, and move on to the next door.

Knock, knock, knock.

A woman answers and greets me with a warm smile—a good sign. I launch into my pitch and hold up a container of Blue Raspberry Crunch Floam.

She tilts her head. "What school do you attend?"

"Golden Valley Middle School, ma'am."

"Have you been selling slime on campus, too?"

The success must show on my face—I'm beaming, knowing I'll beat Meadow. "My business partner and I have placed this remarkable product in the hands of every sixth grader there." I flash a container of globby neon-pink Brain Slime and sweep my hand in front like it's a prize on a game show.

"I see." She nods. "My husband isn't home, otherwise he might want to have some words with you. What's your name again, young man?"

My name? Why would she want to know that? Seems a

little strange. Or maybe she's just formal. I might have to try a different tactic. "I'm Alex Manalo, slime connoisseur, at your service, ma'am. Do you have children in this fine house who'd like to try a sample?"

"I appreciate it very much, Alex, but I'm afraid it's a no thank you. And you may want to hold off from selling at school, too, okay?" Her face relaxes, but still it's a no. Gently she shuts the door.

Hmmm.

I'm waiting at the curb when Logan sprints toward me.

"Let's hit up a few more," I say.

"Okay, but not that one." He points to the house I just went to.

"How come?"

"Mr. Schlansky lives there," he says, and I look at him blankly. It's been two days—I barely remember my home-room teacher's name. "The teacher from school who hates slime? We'd get caught for sure."

Uh-oh. So that's why his wife asked all those questions. Is she going to say anything to him? My stomach does some tumbles. Should *I* say something to Logan? Although even if Mr. Schlansky's wife tells on us, we're not on school grounds so he can't get too mad. We can't get in trouble, right? Right.

"Should we keep going?" Logan asks.

I look down at my watch. Still a little time before soccer. "Let's do it."

By the time we finish a few more blocks, my backpack is lighter and we're feeling good.

"That was the best," Logan says.

Side by side, we walk back to his house. It's been a while since I've heard from Raj. I still miss him, but not as much. He's got new friends, and for the first time it's feeling like maybe I do, too.

The next couple of days go like this: school, sell slime, practice soccer. Rinse, repeat.

On Friday after school, Logan, Carl, Pepper, and I brave the biggest sneaky selling frenzy at the lockers yet. After the last buyers clear out, I unzip my bag and look inside.

"Can you all still come over on Sunday? Because look!" I hold up my backpack and show them the inside—it's empty.

Logan grins and we do our secret handshake.

"Maybe we should do it sooner, like tomorrow?" Carl says.

"Sorry, it's the G-Beatz' first game tomorrow."

"Good luck," Pepper says, and my stomach jumps. Playing still terrifies me even though my soccer team's been practicing a bunch. Still, my slime team smiles. At least I've got this.

IT'S TIME

First game of the season later today and all I can think about is that I don't want to screw things up. I grab Lola's feather duster behind the counter at the store and walk the aisles shaking it around, trying not to think about it.

"Ready, big guy?" Dad asks. "Hey, look, I've got on my good-luck charms!" He pulls his sweatpants up and I see his socks with the soccer balls. He wears them whenever his favorite team plays, and I guess now for our games. Dad's disappointment after that horrible first practice has been replaced by his game-day ritual: pure excitement. He also gets this way before Nick's games.

The door chimes.

From behind the counter Dad says, "So sorry, but we're closed," until he looks up. "Francisco!" He's been coming to the market for years.

"Oh, I didn't realize, John," Francisco says.

"No, come in, come in," says Dad. "It's good to see you, my friend. We've packed up a lot already, but please, get what you need."

Francisco usually grabs lunch to go before his jobs—he's a construction worker. Now he's part of the team fixing up the empty space next door.

"Guess I won't be enjoying any of your lola's adobo and rice today, huh, Alex?" he says to me with a friendly smile.

"Nope, but you're going to love our new menu," Dad says, except he doesn't mention how different it will look.

Francisco grabs a drink from the fridge, and a few other snacks, and pays. "Alex, how's your new school going?"

"School is . . . school," I say, and he laughs. "How's your artwork?" I ask.

Painting landscapes and portraits is Francisco's specialty, and he's trying to start his own business. He's gotten into local shows, and one of his small oil paintings—of a redwood forest not far from here—hangs near our register. On the back he signed it to Lola: *Thank you for always keeping my heart happy and my belly full.* It's one of her favorite things in the store.

"I'm still creating every day," he says. "My stuff may not be hanging in every house yet, but it keeps me happy." He gives us another warm smile.

We say our goodbyes and Dad locks up.

"Almost game time," he says, and my nerves go full blast again. I reach for some putty-slime in my pocket and give a quick squish to calm down.

Let's get this over with.

FAST MOTION

Season kickoff.

A clear sky.

Feet tapping.

A windless morning.

Palms sweating.

Dad and I walk over to the bright green turf. "Remember to call me Coach out there, okay?" he says. "Only when we're on the field."

I nod. "Sure."

For a moment I shut my eyes, wishing and hoping for Dad to keep me out the entire game, but when the team huddles, Dad—I mean Coach Manalo—assigns our positions.

"Alex, defender. Just inside the half line."

Phew. All I have to do is stand in the way of someone who has the ball, which doesn't take as much thought as some of the other positions, which I'm sure he did on purpose. I'm completely fine with that.

I nod back at Dad. The team puts all hands in and we yell, "We're gonna Beatz you!" and run out onto the field.

My heart thumps.

"Hey, Alex, don't forget, the goal's *that* way," says Rudy, cracking up and elbowing Trevor. Coach gives them both a stern look and Rudy holds in his laughter. My teammates don't think I can do this.

Neither do I.

"All right, time to choose captains," Coach says. He points to Trevor—and me. I spoke too soon.

Trevor and I walk toward the referee along with the other team's cocaptains in the middle of the field.

On the sidelines, a field of spectators sit in fancy umbrella chairs, snacking and watching us like a circus. When I mess up they'll see—and they'll wonder why the coach's son can't play. I cringe.

Snap out of it, Alex. We haven't even started yet.

The ref tosses a coin.

"Organic G-Beatz, over there. Unicorn Ninjas, that's your side." The ref points.

We go to our marks.

Kickoff.

The game moves quickly. We're blue, but a green shirt gets control of the ball and a giant boy kicks it down the field. I'm supposed to go after the ball, but the kid runs so fast, he must have magic shoes. I can barely keep up.

People from the crowd shout and cheer and yell advice as if they're the ones playing.

Kick it!

Pass it!

Get in there!

Hustle!

I'm not even sure who they're shouting at. The sunshine hits my eyes and everything looks fuzzy.

Even our coach yells, "Good hustle!" But it's no use, our opponents scored two goals already. We're getting creamed.

Another giant kid in a green jersey rams the ball and I run up to him, but he's quick as a gazelle. He kicks the ball to one of his teammates and it flies near me—by my face—and I try to shield myself, except I touch the ball by accident. In soccer the most basic rule is "no hands." I knew that, but it was instinct to block my head.

"Foul!" the ref shouts.

Trevor, Rudy, and the others scowl at me. The other team gets a penalty kick because of my mistake. They kick the ball in and the game keeps going. Still two to zero.

The other team runs full-speed; I do my job of defending the ball from another player, charging up to him, but he kicks it straight into the net to a mass of cheers. Three to zero. He sticks his tongue out at me and pumps his arms in victory.

"Come on, Alex! Eye on the ball!" yells Trevor.

Please be over now.

The game goes on and the other team scores three more goals. Even though I'm trying as hard as I can, my body aches. With all the running and screaming around me and the sun in my eyes, I'm getting confused. The other team keeps pushing and my team keeps running after them, but I stand there, tired, hands on my knees, breathing hard. Everyone leaves me behind and the game keeps going.

A whistle blows. Halftime. I hate this. I feel my eyes watering.

Don't cry.

Dad replaces me with another teammate for the rest of the game.

"Finally," Rudy says. "Maybe now we can score."

I sit it out, but our team never scores. We lose. Big-time lose.

In my head I hear Lolo's voice telling me winning doesn't matter, but looking around at my teammates . . . everyone knows it does.

We go to the sidelines to regroup while the other team hugs and woots and congratulates each other.

Trevor looks at me and I brace myself for one of his

snarky remarks, but he says: "Good effort, dude." I look around and he's definitely talking to me. "Listen, dribble with your head up. It'll make you go faster."

Even though Coach gives the team a cheery we'll-get-'em-next-time pep talk, I know he's disappointed. So am I.

I KEEP HEARING THAT WORD

It's Sunday morning, which means I start my day with a call to both sets of my grandparents. First are Lolo and Lola, then Nanang and Tatang, before Dad and I head to the store.

"Another big day," Dad says to me after I'm finished on the phone. He's smiling again, even after yesterday's loss, because we've closed the store now, temporarily. It's time to finish getting the new and improved Manalo Market ready. I run out to the car and we drive over. When we get there, Dad hands me a laminated sheet of paper to hang on the door.

"Care to do the honors?" he says.

"Definitely." I tape it up for our loyal customers to see:

SEE YOU IN THREE WEEKS FOR OUR GRAND REOPENING!

Inside, most of the shelves are bare. Boxes are piled high along one wall, and large drop cloths and multiple trays of white paint and rollers and brushes dot the floor.

My cousins, aunt, and uncle are here, too. Auntie turns on some dance music to get us in the mood to move—and work. Luckily, no one's asking me about my first game. I'm sure Dad already told them the bad news.

"Check it out, boys," Auntie says. She holds up a hair thingamabob that's knit in rainbow hues. "Ellie made it for me. Pretty fun, huh? She said the colors reminded her of your mom." I've seen Ellie at the crosswalk wearing her creations. Auntie gives me a big smile.

"Neat," I say.

"Ellie's trying to get her little knitting shop up and running. I wish we could help her somehow. Maybe even give her a little shelf space when we reopen."

"A great idea, sis," Dad says. "Something Anna would have thought of." He looks away but smiles.

Auntie ties her hair up in a ponytail and dusts her hands. "Okay, boys and men, remodel time!" She grabs rollers and hands one to each of us.

"Hold on—before we start, I've got something to show everyone," Dad says. He turns the music down and from behind the counter pulls out a golden placard, which he reads aloud:

"Sandwich Bar."

Sammy laughs. "Sandos? What's that for, Uncle?"

Dad stands it up. "We're going gourmet! Organic, locally sourced ingredients, California farm-to-table—you know, the works. I have an old friend who's a chef now and she's helping me design the menu."

"Can we name one after me and call it the Sammich?" Sammy asks.

"The Hammich Sammich!" I say, and my cousins laugh.

"Terrific idea!" Dad says, and Sammy pats me on the back.

"So the market's going foodie?" Nick asks.

"I'll take a gluten-free Tofurky buffalo meatball wrap with a large organic iced water from a Swiss Alps waterfall where yodeling goats hang out, please," Sammy says, and he and Nick laugh.

"That actually sounds so good," Nick says. "I'm starved."

"Work first, eat later," Auntie says. She dips a roller on a long wooden handle and swoops it up and down the wall so the paint glistens. Dad, Uncle Benny, and my cousins pick a corner and start doing the same.

Is no one paying attention?

"Do Lolo and Lola know about these . . . sandwiches?" I ask.

"It's not bad to try something different, Alex," Uncle Benny says as he paints. "If sandwiches don't work out, we can always go back to the old menu."

"Your uncle's right. It's all in the business plan, buddy," Dad says. "You'll have to trust me on this one."

I keep hearing that word, *trust*, but how does that work when he's making so many changes? "What if Lolo and Lola don't agree?" I ask.

"They'll understand because they want the store to thrive. And ultimately, they're businesspeople. When they first immigrated here they saw a need and they filled it," Dad says. He looks at me. "We have this market to thank for everything we have, Alex. It'll put you through college, just like it did for me and your auntie. Nothing we do here is without good intention."

I look over at my aunt, but she's engrossed in painting. Nick swipes a bit of white paint onto Sammy's arm until their mom notices and tells them to stop. Dad turns back to his task. My cousins have stuck in their earbuds, and Auntie and Uncle concentrate on rolling long, even strokes onto the wall.

The door opens and a couple of kids walk in, a boy and a girl. I've seen them around school, but they aren't in any of my classes.

"Hi, kids. Sorry, we're closed now, but do you need some help?" Auntie asks.

"We're here to buy slime," says the girl.

"Slime?" Dad says.

"It's okay, I'll handle it," I tell my family, and I walk outside with them. "We'll have fresh batches tomorrow—come find me or Logan at the lockers before first bell."

"Cool," the boy says. "I didn't think you could do it, but you're proving me wrong."

"So many people want you to beat Meadow," says the girl.

"They do?"

"We've been watching and we feel like you're one of us, Alex," she says. The girl has a dark hair bun on each side of her head, and now I recognize them—they were watching when Rudy told me I should burn Meadow back with my own video.

"What do you mean?" I ask.

"You're one of the good guys. Meadow and Rudy and Trevor—and all the kids like them . . . they always do stuff to make others feel bad. Why are people like that? So dumb." The girl shakes her head, and her lips tighten.

"Yeah. We want you to shake things up," says her friend. "Show them how the good kids can win, too."

"I'll try," I say, and they leave.

This is starting to feel like a lot of pressure. But it also feels . . . nice? I've never had people I don't know count on me before.

When I go back in, Dad says, "What was that all about?"

Maybe I can get his attention, a little teaser before I finally reveal my big news. "They heard I make awesome slime. Neat, huh?" But he's gone back to painting.

I'll get to tell him and my whole family soon that I won the Slime War. Then they'll all take notice.

ELEPHANT'S TOOTHPASTE

An empty 20-ounce plastic bottle
3% hydrogen peroxide solution
Liquid dishwashing detergent
Food coloring
A packet of active dry yeast
Warm water

Dad's still at the store and Auntie's over at the house with me, helping to organize my grandparents' files. She sits on the floor in their office with boxes and paper all around. I peep in.

Auntie looks up at me with a smile. "Hey, kiddo. What are you up to?"

We haven't talked about yesterday's game—she knows how embarrassed I feel about messing up. I just want to forget about it.

"Is it okay if I have some . . . *people* over from school later?" I still haven't heard Pepper, Logan, or Carl use the word *friends* yet.

She gives me a big smile. "I'm happy you're making new friends. Just like your mom. She had so many—she was the kind of person everyone adored."

Whenever Auntie talks about Mom, I don't want her to stop.

Awhile ago I asked my aunt why Dad doesn't like talking about Mom.

She shrugged and said, "Sometimes our brains do strange things when we miss someone. Have you ever told him how you feel?" I shook my head. "What have I said about that before, sweetie?"

My aunt has this thing about stating your feelings—it was something my mom taught her. Even Nanang says Mom was a Feelings Person. So Auntie always makes my cousins and me share our emotions, which sometimes seems cheesy, but I do it anyway because of Mom. Auntie tries to get Dad to do it, but he never plays along.

The doorbell rings. I run down and fling open the door. Logan's unstrapping his helmet, Pepper's pulling books out of her bike basket, and Carl flips his cape like he's in a show.

"Greetings!" says Carl, mysteriously raising an eyebrow.

"I brought research from the bookstore, just in case,"

Pepper says, holding a tall stack of books that reaches to her chin. "Let's go! Slime's a-wastin'!"

Logan nods. "We've gotta make enough to sell out tomorrow."

I lead them into the backyard. Lola has a beautiful garden lined with pots of pink and purple orchids and a wide patio with a big table to fit our whole family plus more. It's the best sliming spot in the house.

Auntie steps out with some snacks—tasty shrimp chips and boxes of mango juice. "Oh, Logan! It's been so long." She opens her arms wide and he gives her a hug.

"You know each other?" I ask.

"Sammy used to be his babysitter. Logan, honey, you'll have to come by more often now. I know Nick and Sammy would love to see you. Maybe you could come by and you could all kick a soccer ball around." Logan smiles at my aunt.

"Thanks, Mrs. Coloma."

"Okay, kiddos, I'll be upstairs if you need me."

"My aunt's right, you should come over for a game sometime." It could be fun with Logan there.

He shakes his head. "I'm horrible at soccer. It's Trevor's thing, not mine."

"It's okay, I'm horrible, too." I shrug. "Should we do some warm-ups first?" I haven't hosted any slime parties before, and I want to impress them with what I know.

"What are warm-ups?" Logan asks.

"Slime challenges. Your chance to be maker," I tell him.

Carl rubs his hands together. "Let me at that gooey stuff!"

"Maybe I'll just watch?" Logan says.

"Why?" Pepper asks. "This is the fun part."

"Experiments never turn out right for me. But I can record you and we can use them as promo videos," Logan says.

"You can't be invited to a slime party and not make any," Pepper says.

"Don't worry, we'll start with something easy to get us in a sliming mood," I say. "Watch."

I run over to the grass, where I've set up an experiment to whip up some Elephant's Toothpaste. Not quite slime, but still a chemical reaction. It's a showstopper.

My business partners help me pour hydrogen peroxide, dishwashing soap, and a few drops of sea-green food coloring into a bottle.

"Swish it to mix," I tell Carl. He swirls it around with a craft stick, then sets the bottle in the middle of the lawn. In a different container, Pepper mixes a packet of yeast with some warm water. "We have to give the yeast five minutes to activate before the last step."

"Woohoo, snack time!" Logan says. "Hey, here's a challenge. How many shrimp chips can we eat in five minutes?"

Apparently it's a whole bag.

After time's up, I say, "Now we'll pour the yeast mixture into the bottle and step far, far away." I put my arms out wide and herd us back a couple of feet. "Who wants to do the honors?"

Carl points to Logan.

Logan tiptoes over, carefully pours it in, and runs off as the mixture bubbles and erupts from the bottle in a thick, foamy, green mound. We go wild, hooting and laughing, and run over to touch it.

"Epic!" says Pepper.

We try a few other challenges, like blindfolding Carl and making him mix slime. Last night I also made mystery balloons, each one filled with a different ingredient. We snip, dump, and mix, without knowing what we'll get. Pepper squeezes out a glittery turquoise glue that oozes slowly like something in an old horror movie. "Satisfying," she says. Even Logan's into it now. Slime drips through his fingers and he busts up.

"A little like magic, huh?" Carl says. "Take something ordinary and make it unbelievable!" He waves his hands over his slime like when he does card tricks.

I smile. "Why are you so into magic?" I ask him.

"It makes me happy. Like you and your slime." Carl shows me a quarter before making it disappear. He's very convincing.

"Yeah, but we should get it one hundred percent right," Pepper says, opening one of the books she brought. "Let's tackle that drying-out problem now."

"Good idea. I don't want to give out any refunds tomorrow," Logan says, and we look up tips from my laptop and make a few adjustments to our product.

After a while we're slimed out, but we have plenty more batches to sell.

"Last day tomorrow," Logan says.

Pepper pumps her arm into a muscle. "Let's crush it."

ESTABLISHED AND GOOD

Sliming with everyone today was so much fun. After Carl, Pepper, and Logan leave, the doorbell rings. When I peep through the hole I see Sammy's spiky hair, then his big, blinking eyeball. He steps back and sticks out his tongue.

I let him in.

"Perfect. Just the two guys I need," Auntie says, bounding down the stairs.

"Got your text, Mom. What is it?" Sammy asks.

"You boys mind going to the store with me to bring back more filing boxes from the office?"

Sammy begins: "Can I . . ."

"Drive?" Auntie dangles a ring of keys and drops them into his palm. "How about you and Alex open up the store, and I'll be right behind you."

"Score!" Sammy sings. He got his license over the summer and will take any chance to practice.

We drive the few minutes to our market. The parking

lot's almost empty, except for one car. Sleek and smooth in a deep, regal blue.

"Whoa. Sweeeet!" Sammy says. "A Lamborghini!" He pulls into the spot next to it. We get out and slam our doors.

My cousin walks around it and leans in to try to see through the tinted windows.

"Hey, kid, not so close!" a blond guy shouts. He's standing near the empty storefront by our market, with two other guys who look the same. They're youngish, like maybe in college or something, all wearing gray hoodies with a logo stitched on the back.

"Just admiring," Sammy says.

"Then admire from afar," the man says.

Sammy rolls his eyes and walks over to the store. He puts a key in the door, but it doesn't unlock. He tries another, but that one doesn't work, either.

I sit at the curb and wait. Those people keep looking into the empty storefront's window.

"I don't know, man, this strip is dead," says a guy wearing thick black-framed glasses. "I mean, look at it." He points to Manalo Market and says to the others, "What does this place even sell?"

"We need a more established area with more trending businesses," says the blond guy.

Established? Trending?

"Dude, the whole point of this is to find a quiet location

for us to disrupt," the man with the glasses says. "This neighborhood is just so . . . I don't even know. It needs more. I mean, who doesn't want robotic juicers?"

Sammy's still trying to unlock the door. I wish my aunt would get here already.

The man with blond hair looks at me, and then at Sammy. "Hey, kid, what are you doing? The place is closed."

Sammy ignores him.

"Do you even speak English?" the man asks. When Sammy doesn't respond, he says, in a rude tone, "*¿Habla inglés?*"

"Excuse me?" Sammy shakes his head. "I don't speak Spanish. I'm Filipino."

"Whatever. Just leave that place alone, kid," the guy says. "I'll call the cops if I have to."

"This is *my family's* store," Sammy says.

I jump up. "Mine too."

The guys look at us in surprise, but one of them, wearing a baseball cap, shoves his friend's shoulder and says, "C'mon, man, that was so rude." He turns to Sammy and me and gives a kind smile. "Sorry, that was really stupid of him to say. We're just checking this area out."

Sammy scans the parking lot. "If you have questions, ask my mom. She'll be here any second."

"So your family owns this place?" the man in the baseball cap asks. He pulls a wallet from his pocket and hands me and Sammy business cards. BAY AREA ROBOTICS. I notice now

141

what's embroidered on their sweatshirts—a robot arm. It's the business Mr. Santiago showed me and Dad that video about.

These are the people who want to be our new neighbors?

"How long has your store been here?" He looks up at our sign. "The . . . Main-ailo Market?"

"Mah-nah-lo Market," Sammy says. "And it's been here longer than I've been alive."

The blond guy goes up to our window, cups his eyes, and looks in. "It looks like a convenience store."

I think about how Lola always says we work for the community. It's *way* more than that. "Everyone comes here. We sell everything—*including* juice. And Filipino food."

"Filipino food? I don't even know what that is." The blond man's nose scrunches up and he snickers at his friends. "We should buy this wreck, too." He laughs even more.

Excuse me? We're renovating.

My head swirls and I try to think of something to say, but I'm too embarrassed—and mad. I've heard people say things like that to my grandparents or to my dad. It makes me so angry, but I never know how to respond.

Sammy joins me at the curb. "I think Mom gave me the wrong keys."

The men talk among themselves as Auntie walks up. "Sorry, you two, I had to take a quick phone call." She unlocks the door.

I stay outside and watch those people walk around and peer into the other stores.

Before the Kidpreneur awards were announced, I told Lolo how badly I wanted first place. He patted my back and asked, "Did you enjoy yourself?" I nodded. "Did you accomplish your original idea?" I nodded again. "There you go. Success, anak. You don't need first place. It'd be nice, don't get me wrong, but there are other ways to triumph. Don't you think?"

Those guys get into their fancy car and rev the engine. Mr. Santiago called them successful, but I'm not impressed.

WHEN WE WIN

Slime War, last day!

I wake early to pack my bag with all the slime we made.

Nothing can ruin my Monday-morning mood, not even Meadow's scowling face at the crosswalk. She looks straight ahead as I pass, but for the briefest second she glances over. I try to give a smug smile so she knows I'm going to win—but she gives me the same smile first.

I meet Carl, Pepper, and Logan at the lockers.

"Ready?" I rub my hands together.

"To own this place? Of course!" Logan says. He raises his palm and Carl gives him the highest five.

"No matter what happens, we're all in this together," says Pepper.

No matter what happens.

I know I need to stop daydreaming about winning, but my daydreams always turn into Dad being so impressed that he lets me quit soccer to focus on my business. Now, that would be amazing.

"Alex, pay attention," Pepper says, and I snap out of it. A few kids come over and ask for slime. "Step right up!" she tells them. I unzip my backpack and they peek in to make their choices.

We sell in between every period, and finally, at lunch, my team and I sit at a table in the courtyard under a leafy tree. Our last big selling session before the moment of truth, and we still have a steady stream of happy customers.

A boy walks up. "One Butter Slime, please." Logan hands him the container and the kid runs off.

"Should I push the Brain Slime next, or do we still have a bunch of the Taro Teas left?"

I shake my backpack upside down—it's completely empty. "We sold out!"

Carl opens the *Star Wars* tin and shows our riches: stacks of dollar bills wrapped in red rubber bands. Pepper grabs a stack and fans herself. We all worked hard for this, and she and Carl are getting a cut, too.

"Remember when we were little and we used to sell lemonade?" Pepper asks.

"But Carl kept drinking up our profits?" Logan says, and he and Pepper bust up.

Carl shrugs. "What? I was thirsty!"

"Take a look around, everyone," Logan says. "This is our territory now. Once we win, we'll expand."

"To the private schools!" Carl says.

"Then to the high schools!" Pepper says.

"Keep thinking big, my friends," Logan says. "This is only the beginning."

He said "friends," and I've got a grin on my face now.

"No matter what happens, I'm glad . . . I'm glad we did this together and . . . I'm glad I met you all," I say.

"Aww, that's sweet," Pepper says. "Same, Alex."

"And only a little cringey," Carl says, but with a big grin, too. We all laugh.

"Friends," says Logan.

"And forever slimers," says Pepper. She puts her hand in the middle and we stack ours on top.

"For the win!" we say, pushing our hands up to the sky.

It's happening. I've got friends cheering me on, and at lunch I know where to sit instead of worrying like I used to when Raj was home sick from school. My head buzzes and I can feel myself smiling. I can't seem to stop.

"They're coming," Pepper says. She points at Melvin Moore marching toward us with Meadow and her people not far behind.

I clasp my hands together tight. "The moment of truth."

My friends and I stand. Kristina B. hands Melvin a thick envelope, and Logan gives him our *Star Wars* tin of money.

"I shall plant myself over there and discreetly tally the results. Each team send one person from your party to ensure I am tallying the money fairly. And please, I beg of you, keep a lookout for teachers and yard duties." He walks to an empty table. We send Pepper, and Meadow's group sends another kid, and they follow Melvin like bodyguards.

My friends and I sit at one table, and Meadow and her crew are at one across from us. More kids gather.

Carl performs magic for everyone waiting, pulling quarters out of people's ears, and I start to forget about everything . . . until out of nowhere Melvin Moore appears, in between the two groups. Maybe he's the real magician. All our chattering stops.

"Well?" Logan asks.

Melvin looks from Meadow's group to ours.

"It's . . ." Melvin glances from my group to Meadow's.

"Well?" Meadow says.

Melvin shakes his head. "It's a tie."

"What?" I say.

"Friends, my eyes did not deceive!" says Melvin. "Down to the exact dollar! In all my years as a slime historian I have never witnessed or known anything like this."

"How?" Kristina B. says, and she points to Logan. "They cheated."

"No we didn't!" Logan says.

"You went outside of school to sell!" Kristina B. says.

"There's nothing in the rules about going off campus, and you know it. Besides, you were the ones who trashed us with your video."

"It was fair and square," Kristina B. says.

"And dirty!" Logan shouts.

"Calm down. Breathe and release, my peeps," Melvin Moore says, extending his arms like he wants to hug us all.

"You wanna play dirty? I'll show you dirty!" Kristina B. shouts. She grabs an XL vat of slime from a kid sitting next to her, rips off the top, and scoops out an impressive amount of goo. She chucks it at Logan, who ducks, and it splats right on Meadow's face and hair.

Meadow shrieks. "Why did you do that!" She grabs the nearest tub of slime from some other kid and does the same, aiming for Kristina B., but it lands on an unsuspecting boy about to take a big bite of nachos. Carl, Kristina B., Pepper, and Logan start busting up. Suddenly lids pop, hands reach, arms chuck, kids shout, and goo slings—and I'm in the middle watching the chaos.

Slime's flying across tables when I see a grown-up charging toward us. A teacher—Mr. Schlansky.

Oh. No.

"Whatever is going on here—" Mr. Schlansky says at the exact moment a glob of slime smacks him on the forehead.

The entire courtyard goes quiet.

Slowly, he wipes his brow. Mr. Schlansky's face is red and the veins on his forehead pop out like lines on a map. But calmly, he says, "Meadow MacPhearson, Alex Manalo,

Logan O'Grady, Kristina Bolanos—the principal's office. Now." He turns to the rest of the crowd and says, "Nothing more to see here, students. Bell's about to ring. Everyone to your classes."

Logan and I look at each other. We're dead.

COMMUNITY LEADERS

We follow Mr. Schlansky through the courtyard, and a few kids linger to watch.

I'm right behind Meadow and give her shoe a flat tire because I'm walking so close and not paying attention. She turns around and shoots me a death glare, like she'd like nothing better than to sock me.

"That was an accident," I whisper.

"Was getting us called into the office an accident, too?" she hisses, and specks of spit shoot out of her mouth, she's that wound up.

"I didn't do anything."

Mr. Schlansky turns around and we all go quiet. "I'd heard, from a very credible source, that there has been slime on campus." He looks right at me. "And now that I've seen it with my own eyes, this can no longer go on."

"We're sorry, sir," we all say. He keeps walking and we follow.

At the office, there's a row of chairs outside a frosted-glass door with a sign that reads PRINCIPAL RACHEL RAMOS. We each take a seat.

It feels like forever until the door opens. Principal Ramos sticks her head out and I catch a glimpse inside: windows, sunlight, and plants. Maybe this won't be so bad. It certainly seems friendly in there.

"All right, Golden Valley Eagles, in ya come," she says.

There are four seats facing her desk in a semicircle. My thumbs won't stop tapping together.

"Alex, I think you're the only one here I haven't had the pleasure of meeting in person yet." She gives me a warm smile, and my nerves don't feel as bouncy.

"Nice to meet you," I say, because I'm not sure what else to say. Meadow rolls her eyes.

"Okay, responsible sixth graders, let's cut to the chase. You know very well that secret slime operations have been disruptive to our wonderful learning community here."

Logan opens his mouth: "But don't you think we're being innovative and entrepreneurial—"

Principal Ramos holds up her hand. "A persuasive argument, Mr. O'Grady, but this is the final warning. I've learned through multiple sources that you four are the main purveyors of this operation, and that's why I called you in. I need you to be thoughtful leaders. You are to cease selling slime at school. If this happens again, you'll face consequences." I look at the rest of the kids, but they're staring at their shoes. "Does everyone understand?"

We all nod and say yes.

"I've spoken to your parents and guardians and they understand as well. They're responsible for whatever your consequences are at home." She gives us a stern look that turns into a semi-smile. "Kids, I appreciate your entrepreneurial spirit, but not like this and not here, okay?"

We follow each other out, shoulders hunched, no one saying a word as we file down the hall back to our classes.

WHERE I STARTED

Once we're around the corner from the office, Meadow turns to me and Logan: "This was all your fault."

"Ours? How?" Logan says.

"How else would she have found out?" Meadow says.

"We didn't say a word!" Logan says. "Why did *you* have to throw the slime back at Kristina B.? This was just as important to us as it was to you!"

Meadow shakes her head. "I don't know how he found out, but Mr. Schlansky busted us and *you* have him for second period, *Logan.*"

"You've got some nerve—" Logan says.

"Don't blame Logan," I say. "I sold slime at Mr. Schlansky's house."

Logan's and Meadow's eyes get wide. "You did what?" Logan says.

"I didn't know he lived there until after you told me—his wife answered. And I didn't know it was his wife until after. He never even came to the door."

"And you didn't tell me?" Logan says. "I could have tried to fix things."

Kristina B. points to me. "You ruined the whole war! There's no way we can sell slime anymore, not even *behind* the teachers' backs," she says. "It's too risky now."

Meadow's lip trembles. "This was *my* thing, Alex. My school and my slime, and you came in and ruined it!"

"I didn't mean to," I say.

"You're the worst," Meadow says, and she and Kristina B. head to their classrooms.

"I didn't mean for any of this to happen," I say to Logan.

"My parents are gonna kill me if the principal called. Thanks a lot, Alex." He turns to go, too. "It's nobody's territory now." Logan brushes past my shoulder—hard.

"I'm sorry—"

My words echo down the empty hall and I'm left where I started: with nothing.

YOU, DEAR SLIMER, SERVE A PURPOSE

The last-period bell rings, and as I make my way down the halls, heads turn and disappointed looks follow me. I'm stopped by Melvin Moore, blocking my path.

Not him, too.

"I wasn't trying to mess any of this up, I swear," I say.

He puts his hands on my shoulders, looks me in the eyes, and says: "My profuse apologies for once calling you Felix. You have a name. Your name is Alex. Alex Felix Slimanalo. And you, dear slimer, serve a purpose. To bring this school together. Never forget this. And never forget . . . I believe in you."

"Ummm . . . thanks, Melvin. Wow . . ." I stare down at the ground. "That means a lot," I say, but when I look up again—he's gone.

More kids sneak glances my way and glare.

I sprint past the lockers to the bike racks, slip mine out, and pedal away as fast as I can. Once school's out of sight I slow down—I'm in no hurry to get to the market, especially if Dad got a call from the principal. He already seemed stressed out with store stuff, and this will only make things worse.

It's quiet when I walk into the store. Dad's at the counter and fixes his gaze right on me.

Here we go.

"I . . . ummm . . . I'll be in the office!" I say.

"Not so fast, son," he says. "We need to talk."

"Can we do it later? I have a bunch of homework."

"No. I got a call from your school. What's going on, Alex?"

I sigh. "It was a Slime War."

Dad rubs his face and sighs. "I've gotten calls from Pepper's parents and Logan's mom, too. Luckily she already knows our family." Dad's face pinches up. "None of this is a good look for us, Alex."

"Sorry, Dad."

"Tell me in your own words what happened, please."

"I was trying to sell slime . . ." My voice echoes through the store. "But I didn't think I was doing anything wrong. All the kids wanted me to."

"Since when have I ever taught you it's okay to blindly follow the crowd?"

Since team sports. Since wanting me to look like every other kid who has short hair. Since a ton of things—but I don't mention any of that because he seems furious. "I'm putting myself out there, like you wanted," I say.

"Yes, but at school, bud, you need to follow the rules. They exist for a reason."

"I know, I'm sorry."

"I was willing to let you spend money on slime if you tried other activities, but not if it's getting in the way of your studies. Here's what's going to happen." Dad pulls out his clipboard. *He made a list?* "After school, it's straight home for a snack, then to the market to help out until our grand reopening. And no more sliming." He puts down the clipboard. "Logan's mom has the money you all made, and we're going to donate your profits as a group."

I stuff my hands into my pockets. "Does this mean"—I cross four fingers—"no more soccer, too?" *Please let something good come out of this.*

"Slime's off. Soccer's *on.* Do you need me to be any clearer?" I shake my head. "Once the season ends and you've proven you're doing what you should be, you'll regain your privileges. Now head home and finish up your work before practice."

I bike back to the house but turn around midway and go to Logan's instead. His mom answers the door.

"Hi, Mrs. O'Grady. Can I talk to Logan, please?"

She shakes her head. "I'm sorry, Alex, but he's grounded. I'm sure you know."

I peek through the doorway, where Logan sees me—and scowls.

Great.

I RECOGNIZE THAT FEELING

At soccer yesterday, none of the boys talked to me. And at school this morning it's the same thing. Kids pass by with looks and whispers. All the sixth graders know now, and everyone's disappointed.

The bell blares as I grab my books from my locker. I head toward science, and Meadow's in front of the office, handing a bouquet of flowers to Principal Ramos. I can read her lips and it looks like she's saying "I'm sorry."

What's her *deal*?

Pepper's in the hallway. I haven't seen her or Carl since we got in trouble, and I feel guilty for letting them down, too. But she's always been so cool. Maybe Pepper won't care if she's seen talking to the guy who messed up sliming for our whole grade.

I smile and wave. For the quickest second she glances at me like she feels bad, but then she frowns and looks down into a book, walking in the opposite direction.

I trudge to first period. Normally Mrs. Graham's class makes me excited to start the day, but I still have to sit next to the enemy. She's already there. When I take my seat, Meadow turns her back.

Mrs. Graham passes out a worksheet. "All right, partners, please read through this together, ask each other the questions listed, and record your answers in your science journals. Full participation, please! We'll regroup and discuss."

In a few minutes the class is buzzing.

"You want to read first, or should I?" I ask Meadow-Slash-Enemy-Slash-Science-Partner—but she rolls her eyes. I wait for an answer, and she stares down at the sheet. "Well?"

Silent treatment.

I start reading on my own and Meadow does the same, while all the groups around us chitter-chatter. But after a while she says in the quietest voice, "You don't get it, Alex. The Slime War was all I had."

All she had?

Mrs. Graham paces the aisles, checking in with each station. "How's it going?" she asks us.

Meadow's expression morphs into a chipper smile. "Fine, Mrs. G."

We manage to do the worksheet, but as we talk through the questions, Meadow's voice begins to quiver.

I know that wobbly feeling, I've had it lots of times. In my old school when kids made fun of me, sometimes when I wish I had a mom—every time I play soccer. I wonder what's wrong with Meadow.

Lola's always told me that the thing about running a store is, when it comes to customers, you never know who'll walk in. Most are nice and polite, but there are the mean ones, too. The judgey ones. The people who steal. There are those who stiffen when they see that my family doesn't look like them, or that the store carries items they don't recognize, with packaging in different languages.

"If you don't understand someone, try to put yourself in their shoes," Lola has said. "It doesn't mean you should take anything negative—always stand up for what's right and what you believe in—but we grow from learning about others, anak. It's how we make ourselves better. Even from the rude customers I want to boot out of my store—and trust me, I have." She chuckled hard, and I could picture her doing it, too. My grandma's smart and tough.

Something's going on with Meadow.

"Okay, class, time's up!" Mrs. Graham says.

I try to take Lola's advice and put myself in Meadow's situation, but it's hard to imagine anything about her. Although I'd take her glares any day if it meant the Slime War was still on and I still had my friends.

SHE HAS A PLAN

After the longest afternoon, I scan the lockers for Logan, but he's still avoiding me. Finally I spot him in the courtyard and run over, kids all around us, but when he sees me he turns to leave.

"Wait," I say.

"Make it quick." He looks over my head at something far away.

"I wasn't trying to get us caught, I promise." He stares at me coldly.

"Did you hear about Meadow?" he asks. I shake my head. "She has a plan that affects both of us . . . but I don't know if I want to be part of it."

"What is it?"

There's commotion at the bike racks: sixth graders are gathering and whispering, sneaking glances our way.

"Meadow wants to declare a Slimebreaker," he says.

"What happens with a Slimebreaker?" I ask.

"It's never been done, so I don't know exactly—but Melvin Moore will. Even if we did decide to do it, I don't feel like she deserves a second chance, except . . . except I have to save my reputation. Especially with Trevor."

"I guess let's at least go hear what they have to say."

We look at each other. No shake, no smiles. I nod.

IS YOUR PARTY IN?

A pack of kids are hanging around the bike racks, and as Logan and I get closer, the crowd parts. In the middle are Meadow, Kristina B., and Melvin Moore.

"To the park, quickly," Melvin says. "And play it cool, everyone. Cool as this." He points to himself with his two thumbs.

Meadow is stone-faced. She's not giving anything away.

Kids herd across the street in clumps, and Logan and I follow. In the distance I spot the market.

Melvin hops onto a bench as everyone gathers. He holds a finger up and shouts:

"A Slimebreaker has been declared!"

People turn to each other in surprise.

"How can we even do that?" I say. "We're banned, remember?"

"Easy. The park isn't school property," Kristina B. says, and Meadow smiles.

"My dad would kill me if he found out," I say. "I can't make slime, much less sell it anymore."

"But technically we can—because of Mrs. Graham's class," Meadow says. "We all got assigned the same slime unit, so we'll have an excuse to make it. And we won't be selling it at school, so we're not breaking any rules."

Kristina B. says, "The Slimebreaker will happen here—not at GVM—and winner gets territory to sell at the park *and* they control that territory until we're done with middle school. No one else."

"A slimeopoly," Logan whispers.

"Winner takes all," says Meadow. A determined look replaces her weepy one from earlier.

Melvin turns to Logan. "Is your party in?"

Logan turns to me and whispers, "I think we should do it. After we win I'll have my best friend back, and you take over as Slime Hero and start your own business. We both get what we wanted."

Right. What we wanted. I guess Logan was only trying to impress Trevor, but maybe I wasn't that different, wanting to impress my dad. *What do I do?*

I think back. Fast. For someone who started with nothing at a new school, I got far. People know my name. I scan the crowd and see Carl and Pepper and all the kids like me who don't usually get any attention. Little roller coasters go off in my head and travel all the way down to my fingertips and to my toes. Now I know—I'll do this for us. I face the crowd.

"I'm in."

Melvin takes my wrist and Meadow's and yanks our arms up high.

"I declare a Slimebreaker!" Everyone cheers. Melvin clears his throat and announces new rules: "Team Meadow and Team Alex, your goal is to come up with one perfect batch of slime. Please package your concoction in a clear container without your name and give it to a neutral party, who will bring it to me. Each batch will be tested by nine randomly selected slimers, none of them from Golden Valley Middle. These judges shall vote by a marble dropped into a hat for their favorite. The hat with the most marbles wins. Victor takes full slime-selling territory here at the park for the rest of their time at GVM. If the situation eases at school with admin, the boundaries will be extended to campus. Easy peasy, fresh and slime-squeezy."

"Who's Victor?" Carl asks, but no one pays attention.

"Three weeks from today, we meet back at this same spot," Melvin says. "That gives you time to formulate your best art possible, and gives me ample opportunity to find suitable, nonbiased judges. Sliming is not my only passion, you know. I also play the accordion. Now. You two." He points to me and Meadow. "Shake."

We extend our hands and grip so tight we both know we're serious.

One more chance.

BLUE WAVE

1/2 cup of clear or white glue
1/2 cup of water
1/4 cup of liquid starch
Royal-blue food coloring

Slimebreaker, here we go. I tape Mrs. Graham's project sheet above my bedroom wall for proof, in case Dad walks in. Whatever I make for the tiebreaker, I'll use for Mrs. Graham's assignment, too. If Dad ever questions it, I'm covered.

I swipe ingredients down from my shelf. "Okay, Alexander Timothy Manalo, let's do it!"

I used to think motivational talks, especially to yourself, seemed weird, but they made us do them during Kidpreneur. We learned that basketball players who give themselves pep talks before a game end up passing the ball around faster, so maybe it works. At this point I'll try anything.

I grab a big bottle of glue and glug some out, but the jug nearly flies out of my hands because the container's so light. It's almost empty.

Shoot!

I need more supplies.

"Alex!" I hear Nick calling outside. I run downstairs to find him and Sammy at the front door. Nick's carrying a neon-pink soccer ball under his arm.

"Let's go, Lil A," Nick says.

"Where?" I say.

Nick yanks on my arm and pulls me outside toward the car. "Stop asking so many questions."

"We're here to help," Sammy says. "And I got the keys!" He jangles them.

"We want to show you some pointers for your next game," Nick says.

"Dad told you how bad we lost, huh?"

"You know how Uncle John *loves* giving replays," Nick says, and rolls his eyes. Uncle Benny's the same, and he and Dad aren't even blood-related.

"I don't want any pointers," I say. "You know I'm not a soccer kid. I just want to make it through the rest of the season without getting killed by a monstrous, overgrown twelve-year-old."

Sammy laughs but then says, "So tell your dad you don't want to play."

I shake my head. "That would never work. He already knows I don't want to."

"Then quit talking and let's get you as good as the rest of your team," Nick says, seriously. He's right. If I have to keep playing, I don't want to keep embarrassing myself on the field.

"Only if you take me to the dollar store after?" I say. I can stock up for Slimebreaker.

"Deal," Sammy says.

"I call shotgun," Nick says, and we all get in.

THE MORE YOU DO IT

Sammy drives us to their school and rap music thumps out the windows as we cruise through our neighborhood. We reach Golden Valley High, which looks like the middle school, same color scheme and kiosk and everything, but five times as big.

"All you have to do is focus on the ball," Nick says. "Just keep trying. The more you do it, the better you'll get. It's like anything else."

I can do this.

We run drills on the grass. At first I'm not into it, but with my cousins, it doesn't feel like a chore. We run and laugh until we're out of breath, and I don't think they're judging my every move the way my dad and the boys on my team do. My cousins don't care how well I do at this stuff—they never have. Maybe that's why they feel like brothers.

My cousins practice kicking the ball toward me, but

every time, I protect my face. A bruised eye from a hurtling ball does not sound fun.

Nick runs up to me. "Hey, I wanna try something. Go stand way over there." He points to the end of the field. "We're going to work on your goalie moves."

"Are you kidding?" I say. Doesn't he know my chances of getting smacked in the face by the ball are infinitely higher as a goalkeeper?

"If I know Uncle, you'll have to play it at some point," Nick says. "Remember that summer he coached my team?" I nod. "Plus you're totally good at shielding yourself whenever the ball comes near. I think we can use your instinct to your advantage. Come on, let's try."

Sammy and Nick make me stand several feet away as they kick ball after ball toward me. On the first few I cover my head and duck.

"Wuss!" Sammy yells.

Nick holds up a ball and points to it. "Focus on this. The key is to anticipate where it will go, then block it. I repeat. If you don't want the ball to hit you, block it." He sprints over and demonstrates how to jump up and reach. I feel silly leaping around—especially with Sammy, who does a little butt-shake dance whenever I do—but I let Nick show me how.

Nick runs back to his spot and I take a big breath. Maybe they're right? If they've got it in them, and they're family, then so do I. Manalo blood. We're winners.

I take my position. Sammy runs forward and kicks the ball and it hurtles toward me. I jump. The force of the ball pushes me back—but I've caught it!

"Nice!" Sammy shouts.

As they kick ball after ball toward me—hard—they're full of advice:

"Look for the ball, not your opponent!"

"Don't wait on the line!"

"Don't lock your elbows!"

"Take control!"

Miraculously, I start to get the hang of it, reaching and diving and blocking that ball.

"Not bad, Alex!" Nick shouts as I finally block one without flinching. It was still scary, but I did it. And bonus: I didn't get hit.

Soon they're not even going easy on me, kicking the ball my way with force.

We end our training at In-N-Out, scarfing down burgers and shakes and fries.

"Want to hear something funny?" Nick asks.

"Sure," I say.

"During my first match freshman year I was trying to impress Mikayla Khan before Spring Fling. But I tripped over my feet and almost landed in dog poop. I was so embarrassed that I cried like a baby in front of Mikayla and the whole school!"

Sammy cracks up. "She never went to any dances with him."

"But . . . it's okay," Nick says. "Sometimes you just gotta feel what you gotta feel, you know? And if soccer's not your thing, it's okay to tell your dad. Uncle will get over it."

What he's saying makes sense, except something happened today I never would have expected: I did it. I got through our practice and actually did okay.

Right there, over a Neapolitan shake from the secret menu, I make up my mind.

"I'll stick with it."

I want to prove I can do this—and not just for Dad anymore. For myself.

Sammy leans over with a sneak-attack head noogie. I bust up and a fry shoots out of my mouth.

"Awesome. Then I'll keep helping you," he says, and Nick agrees.

We leave the restaurant and get back in the car. Sammy drives toward home.

"Can we go to the dollar store now?" I ask.

"Sure," Sammy says. When we park there, my cousins get out of the car with me.

"Actually, I can walk home. It's not far."

"Why?" Nick asks.

"Please? It's easier for me to get stuff by myself." I flash them my best pleading look—I don't want them telling

Dad what I buy. "I'll only be a little while, I need some things for school. You know I come here all the time on my own."

"Whatever you want, little cuz," Sammy says. "Text us when you get home."

THEY DON'T UNDERSTAND

Without Dollar Dreamz I'd never be able to slime so much—they've got everything I need, and it's not as expensive as a regular craft store. Everything costs a buck no matter what it is.

First, shampoo. I head toward the back rows, where they have it in every brand, scent, and color. If I'm going to win Slimebreaker, I need to add my own touch, so I have to start with a neutral base. I'm looking around for inspiration when I hear someone familiar.

"Mom, please?"

"No, Meadow. We don't need it."

I sneak a glance down the aisle. It's Meadow and a woman who looks like her, probably her mom.

Ugh.

Meadow's getting ready for the Slimebreaker, too.

"But Mom, I do need this," she says. Her mom puts the shampoo back on the shelf.

"What we *need* is toothpaste, Meadow. And food. I know this is hard, love, but we can't throw money away."

"I get it, okay?" I can hear Meadow's sigh even from the end of the row.

Meadow's mom rounds the aisle toward the registers. I'm about to slip away, but Meadow spots me. She's crying.

"What are you doing here?" Her eyebrows narrow and her face tightens.

"Same thing you are." I hold up shampoo bottles. I try to smile, but her voice is shaky again, like during Mrs. Graham's class. Whatever she and her mom were talking about sounded kind of serious.

She wipes her tears away. "My mom doesn't think I should be wasting money on slime. Please don't tell anyone."

"If it makes you feel any better, my dad hates me sliming, too."

"Why?" she asks.

"I don't know, he only wants me to do the things he approves of. Things he was into when he was my age. He's so weird about that stuff."

"Why do parents get that way? I'm trying to help my mom by selling slime . . . but . . . she won't even listen to me."

"They don't get it," I say.

She shakes her head. "They never do."

Our eyes meet for a quick moment, but she looks away and walks back toward her mom.

"Hey, Meadow?" I say, and she turns back.

"Yeah?"

"Thanks."

"For what?"

"For thinking of the Slimebreaker. It was smart." I mean it. I didn't want to lose all that good energy we were building.

"Like I said—it's all I have."

I look at her for a second, but Meadow's eyes don't meet mine.

Her mom peeks around the corner. "Let's go, Meadow."

Meadow looks at me. "See you at school," she says.

I grab some glue and finish shopping. On the walk home my phone buzzes with a text from Logan. He wants to know if I have any of my Slimebreaker batch ready yet, and I send him a thumbs-up.

K. Bring big vat. New idea of how we win.

I perk up. Maybe this means we can get things to where they were before, even if it's just the tiniest bit. We don't have to be best friends, but I miss what we almost had.

FUTURE SLIME KING

The next morning I scan the schoolyard for Logan, with a big container of my latest Slimebreaker trial in my backpack. This batch is bright pink and smells like bubble gum. I don't see Logan anywhere. When I get to science he's already sitting at his station talking to Trevor, but neither of them looks my way. Once the period ends I try to get his attention, but he bolts out the door before we can talk.

During PE, Coach Siena has us out on the field.

"It's soccer time, Eagles!" she says. I can't escape it. Trevor's in this class, too, and he gives a *woot!*—some of the kids laugh. "Who'd like to volunteer as team captains? I'll take four and we'll switch off." Hands go in the air, including Trevor's. I wait next to Logan while teams get picked, but we're not able to say much.

Trevor stands in front of the class. "First player—Future Slime King." He smiles and points toward Logan and me. Logan smiles back and starts to walk forward. "Oh, really sorry, L-man, I meant Alex." Trevor looks at me and I look at Logan, who frowns and steps back. It's several kids until Logan gets picked, and not by Trevor.

We start to play, and I actually know what I'm doing. There are a couple of kids from the G-Beatz in this class, too, but also a lot of kids who, like me, probably haven't played many sports before. It seems like Logan's one of them, because he looks bored standing with his hands on his hips, not running or following the ball.

PE ends and everyone heads back toward the locker rooms. I catch up to Logan and Trevor.

"Nice moves, Alex. You're on fire," Trevor says with a grin, and he raises his hand for a high five. I slap his palm in return. "See you guys at lunch." He runs ahead.

"So what's your plan?" I ask Logan.

"I want to show your slime to some testers and get some feedback after school."

"Smart," I say.

Neither of us says anything as kids rush past to their next class.

"Can I tell you something?" I say.

"It's fine, Alex, don't worry about it. I'm not that mad anymore. We've still got a chance," he says, and takes off, shouting, "Trevor! Wait up!"

I guess Logan's getting what he wanted. And I guess it's all business from now on.

BEST IDEA

The courtyard's packed. I'm searching for a table when I hear a girl's voice shout, "What's for lunch, Farty McFly? Slimeboogers on a sesame seed bun?"

She means me. Of course.

Laughter follows, and I try not to turn around to see who said it, but it's hard to ignore. I catch Pepper and Carl at their own table with a few other kids, watching. There are a bunch of people around, but I don't know who said it.

"Leave him alone, Alex makes awesome slime," says a boy's voice. It's Trevor. He yells, "Ready for our big game this weekend?" I half shrug. "Hey, come sit with us!"

Raj would have called this a pinnacle moment, getting invited to the best lunchtime table. But my feet? Frozen.

I shift my weight from one leg to the other. "Yeah . . . I'm ready. Are you?"

Trevor waves me over and I'm not sure what to do. I try to see if Pepper and Carl might let me join them, but they're back to their other friends, talking and laughing. About me, probably.

Finally my brain makes my feet move. Kids nearby watch as I go sit with Trevor and his friends.

Logan and Rudy sit by Trevor's sides, but neither of them says anything as I set down my lunch. Rudy sneaks a glance at me like I'm not welcome.

"You've gotten really good at soccer. I'm super impressed," Trevor says.

"Thanks," I say.

Trevor keeps talking while the other boys laugh at his jokes or agree with everything he says, even Logan. I can see why they like him. He has this way when he talks, nodding and laughing, saying *hey* to kids when they pass. People always give him a huge smile back, like they're happy he's talking to them. He's that confident out on the field, too. The other tables keep glancing over, the way I used to at my old school at certain kids sometimes because I felt a little jealous, or just plain curious. Rudy's trying to lead the conversation, too, but the boys react mainly to Trevor. Rudy rolls his eyes.

"Hey, you know the Radioactive Raspberry you made?" Trevor says to me. "It's so cool—like rubber!"

"Yeah, we chucked a piece and it smacked that nerd over there between the eyebrows!" says Rudy. Everyone but me laughs, even Logan. Tiny bits of food spray out of Rudy's mouth.

The kid they're making fun of can sense it. He glances everywhere but at us, and looks a little like he might cry. I try to give Logan an eye signal, like *Stop!*—but he still laughs and goes along with it.

Trevor punches me lightly on the shoulder. "So what's the deal? Are you still mad?"

"At . . . at what?" I ask.

"At Meadow's video!" He shakes his head. "That was harsh."

"*And* hilarious," Logan says.

Why's Logan acting like this?

My hands tremble, so I sit on them. I exhale softly and try to picture calm things: walking through tall redwood groves, cold ocean waves crashing, slime stretching silky and wide. My body relaxes a little.

"Nah. It was no big deal," I say. "You've got to come up with smart strategies for your PR to work and not take the easy road." I don't exactly know what I'm saying, but I try to make it sound like I do. They're things I've heard my dad say on conference calls.

"What if she makes another one for Slimebreaker?" Rudy turns to Logan. "Alex should get her back somehow. So you guys can actually win."

"Totally," Trevor says.

"Best idea," says Logan. I catch Logan's eye for a moment and try again to give him a look, but he glances away.

"You could figure something out that's not too awful," Trevor says. "Just something that tells her you're serious about winning."

"Yeah, like putting real boogers in slime and giving it to her as a good-luck gift," Rudy says, and the others laugh like hyenas.

"No, that's stupid," Trevor says. "Where's the strategy in that?"

"What? You think you know better?" says Rudy, and he stares Trevor down, like a challenge.

"Sure I do. Alex needs to think . . . bigger."

Rudy shakes his head. "Whatever."

"Yeah, like . . . ooh, I know!" Trevor leans in and lowers his voice. "Sabotage."

Now Rudy smiles. He raises an eyebrow. "How?"

"Easy," Trevor says. "Meadow buys all her ingredients at Dollar Dreamz, right? My brother works in their stockroom and I know for a fact they don't get warehouse shipments this week—it's every other week. So, go in there and buy all the slime stuff so she can't find what she needs. I heard Meadow telling Kristina B. she's making a supply run today."

"What, Alex is just gonna spend all his money buying hundreds of ingredients off the shelves? Be real." Rudy snorts, and this makes the other boys laugh.

"Buy up the glue. Can't be that much," Trevor says,

with confidence. "Only to stall her a little." He looks at me. "Logan and I will help you. After school, the three of us."

I stare at my food. Is this what people think winning's all about?

"You'd never do that, Trev. You're too chicken," Rudy says.

"You wanna bet?" Trevor says. "Because how cool would it be if my new friend Alex took territory? Alex and Logan, my slime-azing best buddies." He drapes his arms over our shoulders. "We three would rule."

"Three?" Rudy shoots Trevor a death stare.

Logan laughs, but I know it's his nervous laugh. "Yeah. We three would own this place!"

Now I'm not sure why I've ever felt jealous of boys like Trevor and Rudy.

"Trev, you don't have the guts," Rudy says, and Trevor's face tightens.

"Says who?" Trevor's voice drops. I bite my lip as I watch them. "Alex, meet me at the racks after last period," Trevor says. "You too, Logan."

"We can't," Logan says. "Alex and I are testing slime after school. We already planned it. Sorry."

"Plus there's practice later," I say to Trevor.

I try to catch Logan's attention so he knows I'm thanking him for getting us out of this—I can't imagine he wanted to do it—but Logan only looks at his best friend. "You want to come with us, Trev?"

"Sounds boring," Trevor says. "We'll figure out a different time for the sabotage. Me, you, and Alex."

"Told you he wouldn't," says Rudy to the rest of the boys, and they all laugh again.

I want to leave, but I'm not sure how.

"So what's the best prank you guys ever played on someone?" I finally ask. Distraction method!

I launch into how Lola hates cockroaches so I bought a huge bag of fake plastic ones and put them all over the market. "She screamed so loud the other store owners rushed over. But she got me back. Sprinkled them around my bed one night while I slept and I freaked out when I saw them the next morning."

The boys crack up, and they start telling their own stories. No one brings up the sabotage idea again, and I feel like I can breathe easier. For the rest of lunch Trevor jokes with me, shares his chips, nudges my side. Logan tries to act like he doesn't notice, but he keeps glancing over. Kids around us at other tables watch, too, like maybe they're a little jealous, including Pepper and Carl, who look away when I catch their eyes. All the times Raj and I wanted to be part of a group like this, I thought somehow our lives would be better, but now I can't tell if it's worth it.

WE ALL RACE

After last period, Logan and I twirl our combinations and slam open our lockers.

"Tell me more about your slime testing idea," I say, as businesslike as I can be.

"I found some experts from another middle school. They're going to do a slime-blind test: your slime versus store-bought, and they'll play with all of it. We'll ask them to choose their favorite, and if they don't like yours, we'll find out why."

"A little R&D. Research and development. Brilliant," I say. I don't know why we didn't think of it sooner.

"Where's your sample?"

I hand him the large tub of pink slime, which he separates into three smaller containers before we head for the park.

We look both ways before crossing the wide street, and Logan yells: "Race you!" He jets across fast, and so do I. At the curb, we're out of breath and laughing. For a second it feels like how it used to.

But the conversation from lunch is still in my head.

"Can you believe what Trevor wanted to do?" I say.

He shrugs. "I don't know. Meadow's been doing mean stuff to people since kindergarten. Maybe it's not such a bad idea. Trevor still wants to do it. He asked me about it again last period."

"He did?" I say.

"I really want to win this, Alex." He looks at me and puts his fist out.

All everyone talks about now is how to win. But if I lose, will everyone just hate me again? Or ignore me? Maybe if I stay quiet, Logan and the other boys will forget about the sabotage.

I knock my fist into his, then point to a table with a few kids. "Is that them?"

"Yeah. Come on."

Logan introduces me to Janae, who's blowing bubbles with her gum; Oliver, who's expertly turning a Rubik's Cube in quick, fast movements; and Riley, who's timing Oliver on the cube and when a ding goes off, says: "Thirty seconds! Amazing! You beat your last score!" All three kids high-five each other.

Janae gets up from the table. "I'd like to be the first to shake your hand. We've got similar sliming origins."

"We all go to Westward Middle," Oliver says.

"And we've had a Slime War, too," says Riley.

Janae pulls the gum out of her mouth and aims for a trash can. She smiles when it makes it right in. "Let's get sliming."

"On it," Logan says, and from his backpack he pulls out three plastic mats and places them on the table in front of each kid before shaking out containers of different slime in every hue. No labels, so our testers won't know which one is mine.

Oliver opens them all and dumps them onto the mat in a straight line, squishing and pounding each one and laughing with glee.

Janae lines hers up neatly and plays with each batch in the same exact way—stretch-pull-squish, stretch-pull-squish.

Riley looks serious and opens one, sniffs and smells, stretches and pulls. She opens the next and plays with each batch a little differently.

I feel like game show music should be playing in the background.

"We don't want to pressure you, so we'll be over there," Logan says, and he sprints toward the playground. I walk slower behind him, remembering this is where I used to play with my cousins. There's a sandpit, a few swings, and a giant slide.

When fifth grade ended it bummed me out knowing that middle school wouldn't have recess. Yeah, there's lunch, but there's no playgrounds. Some kids don't care, they think playgrounds are babyish—but I still love them.

Logan plops himself onto an empty swing seat, and I do the same, and soon we're pumping as high as we can. We don't say much, keeping to our own thoughts as we move through the sky.

After a bit, Janae waves her hands and we jump off and head back.

Our testers have closed the containers. I bite my lip.

"Okay, I'll start," Janae says. Slowly, she takes away the purple and teal slime and pushes forward the pink one. My smile wants to turn into a giant yell, so I clamp my lips.

"Riley?" Janae says. Riley plonks a vat of green in front of me.

"You're up," Riley says to Oliver.

Oliver slides a vessel of purple forward—but takes it back and chooses the pink.

Logan punches his fists into the air. "Two out of three, not bad!"

The kids say nice things and ask me questions only true slimers can, like what is my ratio of ingredients and how did I come up with the recipe. And we pick their brains about what they liked about my slime and what they didn't. My head spins with ways I can spiff up my Slimebreaker batch.

Janae points to the playground and says, "I haven't played there in a long time . . ."

"Let's go, then!" I say, and that's when the business part stops. We race to the park, laughing, our slime left behind on the table, stacked like trophies.

I bet winning will feel nice, but there are some things that still feel nicer.

LUCKY SHOT

Today's slime testing gave me a burst of good feelings, and I'm trying to hold on to them until practice begins this afternoon. I'm getting a little better with all the extra coaching from Sammy and Nick, but I'm still the least-experienced player.

Dad and I get to the field, where some of my teammates are already concentrating on sprinting back and forth across the turf.

We huddle up. Dad-Coach starts with a new *I believe in you!* speech. "Two games this weekend, we've got this," he says, before getting us all moving.

After a few drills, he tosses bright orange jerseys to half the team, and the rest of us stay in our street clothes for our scrimmage. "Shirts versus jerseys, let's go!"

Even though it's only practice, my hands start to quiver. Now I have to prove myself.

Our match starts and the ball comes toward me. I swipe

it away from the other player with some footwork I learned from Sammy and Nick. I dribble it quickly toward the right goal this time and shoot. The goalie misses and it zooms straight in.

What?

"Lucky shot!" Rudy shouts, wiping his forehead with his orange jersey. I look over at Dad, but he's staring at his clipboard. The one time I score.

"Okay, G-Beatz, let's change it up," Dad says, and he assigns everyone different positions. "Alex, goalie."

"Goalie? Yeah, right," Rudy says, just loud enough for the other boys to hear but not Dad, and the boys laugh.

We take our places.

The other team gets control of the ball. The shooter wallops the ball toward me at full speed. I do what my cousins showed me: eyes on the ball.

I jump like I'm flying and block the goal.

It worked?

"Nice job!" Trevor yells. We're both in the shirts group. I give him a thumbs-up.

The scrimmage goes on. The other group shoots two balls in a row and I do all the right things, blocking both. I look over to Dad, and now he's paying attention.

Our game ends, and I've blocked every ball that hurtled my way—five of them—without flinching or getting scared or feeling like I wanted to throw up.

On the drive home Dad says, "Excellent effort today, Alex. I had no idea you had goalkeeper in you."

"Nick and Sammy are good coaches," I say.

Sure, no one will come knocking on my door for scholarships like Sammy, but I sort of know what I'm doing now.

"You can keep trying goalie, if that feels okay to you?"

"Yeah. That sounds good," I say.

I stick my arm out the window and the wind cools me down.

"Before we get home I have to swing by the store for a quick sec," he says.

When we get there, Auntie greets us with a bright smile. "Hey, boys! I think I've finished with all of Mom and Dad's files."

"You're amazing, sis," Dad says. "Thank you."

"Anything for this place." She lovingly pats the counter.

I'm going to get some rice candy when I see that Dad's hung the store's first dollar back up. It's in the corner tucked away behind the register, where no customer would ever see it.

I point. "Hey, Dad, why isn't Paolo's dollar back in its old spot?"

He shrugs. "We needed some wall space. Hey, Gina, did my package come?"

"Sure did." Auntie hands a cardboard box to Dad and he gives a happy little yelp.

"What's in there?" I ask.

He smiles at me. "The 'something' that we need the wall space for." Dad finds scissors and slices the box open. "There's a larger version coming for the exterior." He cups his mouth and makes trumpet noises—*pum-pada-pum!*—and pulls out a sign:

m market

Dad's grinning and wiping the sign with his sleeve. "I think they left out some letters?" I say. "And the capitals, too."

"Exactly. I got a designer to help—thought we'd go for a little something more modern."

Auntie's face wrinkles. "The 'm market'? It's pretty different."

"We talked about trying new things, remember? I'm just doing a little A/B testing. Throwing it all at the wall and seeing what sticks," he says.

Auntie's face relaxes. "Well, I know how much thought you've put into this, John. I say go for it."

"Shouldn't we . . . take a vote or something?" I say. "It seems like . . ." I'm having a hard time finding the right words.

"It's a fun logo, isn't it?" Dad says. "I love how different it is."

"I . . . I don't know," I say.

"Do you have another suggestion?" he asks, like he's expecting me to give some life-changing idea.

"Never mind." He wouldn't get it.

193

"Remember this business tactic, buddy. If you have complaints, be ready with suggestions for solutions." Dad ruffles my hair. "Let's give it a month to see how the rebranding goes before deciding anything. Nothing's permanent. Besides, I paid for this cool sign already."

"Sounds reasonable," Auntie says.

I'm not so sure.

THE KIND OF ENERGY

My whole life I've heard that my family's store is our pride. It's something we've built, something we own, something that's brought us joy. But now Dad's talking about sandwiches and weird logos?

I lie on my bed and grab my phone from the nightstand. I tap the screen a few times until my grandpa's face pops up round and big and brown on-screen. He's wearing sunglasses, and his gray hair flutters along with the tall palm fronds behind him. Waves roar in the distance. He's on a beach somewhere in Hawaii, and I can almost smell the ocean, salty and crisp.

"Alex, anak!" he says.

"Hey, Lolo! How's Maui? How are Nanang and Tatang?" My mom's parents—they're visiting with them during their trip.

"They're as good as ever—you better call them, too!"

"I will." We video call every week.

"And Maui is perfection. Tough life here." He raises a glass to me in the shape of a tiki face with a hot-pink umbrella poking out and takes a sip. "I wish we'd sold these things at the market." Lolo laughs.

"Hoy! Let me see my anak!" says Lola, and her face slides into view next to his. She takes off Lolo's sunglasses. "Let him see your handsome face," she says, before putting them on top of her own head of wavy gray hair. Lola raises her tiki glass and smiles at me. "My sweet Alex, I miss you, honey-bunny. How's school? Are you eating okay? You look so skinny! I'll cook for you when we get home, anak! How's everything?"

I sit up. "Things are . . . they're really good, Lola. Super fantastic!" I'm smiling big because I'm happy to see their faces, but also I don't want them to suspect anything's off and get too concerned.

Lola eyes me. "What's wrong?"

"What?" I say.

"You've got on the same worried face your father makes. You can't fool me, anak."

"Nothing's wrong, I've just been, well . . . I've been thinking about how we can make the store even better. I mean, not that it wasn't great before, but . . . Dad and I want to give it a final push before we reopen."

Both of my grandparents smile at me now. "The simple fact that you're feeling this way makes it better," Lola says with a nod.

"And it makes us proud," says Lolo.

"Yeah, but . . . it seems like Dad wants to change lots of things. Did he tell you any of his new ideas yet?"

"For instance?" says Lola.

"What we carry, what it looks like, the ceramic elephants . . . all of it!" Everything pent up inside me tumbles out. They nod and listen.

My grandparents turn to each other, Lolo with *his* worried look—I know because it's the same as Dad's. Even through the screen I see his forehead extra wrinkled up.

"Rosa, maybe we should call John and talk to him about it?" he says to Lola, but she shakes her head.

"What did we talk about, Petronilo? Trust." She places a hand on Lolo's cheek and his expression softens a little. She turns back to me. "These changes, Alex, how do they make you feel?"

I shrug. "I like some of them, but some I don't. I felt like I needed to tell you."

"Your dad wants to infuse new life into the store. It's what the market deserves," she says with her warm smile, and I wish I could reach through the screen and hug my grandma.

"But how do we know if what we're doing is best?" I ask.

"You don't," Lolo says. "Everything starts with nothing, anak. So you work with your ideas, you take chances . . . you research and test things out, change things up if you need." Now he's smiling. "I used to give away lollipops when kids came in, but they weren't as excited as when I gave out rice-paper candies. Wouldn't have known if I hadn't tested it out."

"Do you remember the story of how we opened our market, anak?" Lola says. I've heard this story many times, but it's my favorite when Lola tells it. She pats Lolo's plump belly. "Because of his stomach." Lola cracks up.

He takes her hand and kisses it sweetly. "I loved being in our new country with my beautiful family, but I was hungry for a taste of home."

"He wanted patis," Lola says, and she lets out another roaring laugh.

Patis is a salty fish sauce that tastes much better than it smells—I like mine on rice with tomatoes and fish flaked all over. "You're making me hungry," I say.

"Exactly," he says. "We couldn't find the ingredients we needed to make our beloved dishes."

"And oh boy, was I tired of hearing Mr. Grumpy complain," Lola says. "So I took charge and told him we'd open up our own sari-sari store, but California-style."

"It was the hardest challenge we've ever had but the most rewarding," Lolo says.

"And don't forget the market helped us become the best party hosts in town!" adds Lola. "We met so many people who've become great friends. Remember all those barbecues when you were little? Bring the same energy back."

My grandparents look at each other for a long pause. "Thank you, my love, for helping me to remember," Lolo says to Lola, his frown completely gone now.

They raise their glasses and toast. It's cute when they get all gushy. I can see their love.

"Alex, it's good to start with the past. We have to understand it to know how to move forward," Lolo says.

"You and your father will bring back the neighborhood party, I guarantee," Lola says with a firm nod. "So whatever trouble or problems you're having with the store . . . leave us out of it! We're retired now!" They start laughing uncontrollably.

"She's joking, anak, but your dad's been hard at work. Have faith in what you both know, okay?"

They make it sound so easy.

LET'S WIN

When I find Logan at school the next morning, he's grabbing books from his locker. Trevor's by his side, like they're best friends again. I walk to my locker and Trevor calls over to me.

"We're gonna make it to the finals. I can feel it," he says.

I slam my locker closed and walk over to them. "You know it," I say.

Some girls pass by and flash smiles at Trevor. One of them says hi to me, too, but I've never seen her before. "I bet he'll win the Slimebreaker," she says to her friend as they walk away. I can feel myself blushing.

Logan looks from me to Trevor. "I'll come watch, Trev," Logan says. "You'll win it for your team, for sure."

"Only if we have this dude blocking every goal." Trevor flashes me his golden smile and puts his hand out for a high five. I catch Logan rolling his eyes.

The only thing I keep hearing about now is winning. Dad,

Trevor, my cousins, my teammates—they all want G-Beatz to win. Then there's Logan, who wants to win Slimebreaker so badly. I'm starting to get tired of it. The G-Beatz have gotten good—we've only lost one game. Somehow we gelled, like when slime bonds together as a chemical reaction of different ingredients to make something even better. So maybe we'll win, but what happens if we don't? How's everyone going to feel then?

Logan, Trevor, and I head into Mrs. Graham's class. She's wearing a T-shirt of a cat holding a bone that says I FOUND THIS HUMERUS and has her I've-got-a-good-project-for-us-today grin, which makes me want to settle everyone down so we can start. Pretty soon we'll get to bring in our slime.

"We're trying something different this morning, gang," she says. "Some team-building! You're paired with your station partner." A few kids groan, and Meadow just looks at me like it's the last thing she wants to do right now. "Each team will get a stack of plastic cups, and your challenge is to build a tower without using your hands, only using this device." She holds up a rubber band with two strings attached. "But here's the catch. You'll be timed—two minutes—and you and your partner can't talk to each other when you're building."

"I'll grab the stuff," Meadow says, and we set everything up at our station.

Once the class is ready, Mrs. Graham starts the timer.

Meadow and I go for it. We stack a few cups, but they

fall. When I want to go in one direction, she wants to go in the other. I glance around, and everyone else is so much further along. "Eyes on the tower," Meadow whispers, and Mrs. Graham reminds us that we can't speak.

"Time's up in three . . . two . . . one!" our teacher says, and everyone puts their hands up, laughing. We're the only ones who didn't build a full tower.

Meadow shakes her head. "We could do better."

"Agreed," I say.

"We'll do this one more time," Mrs. Graham says. "Partners can talk first about how to improve."

"Let's beat everyone," Meadow whispers mercilessly. She's intense—at everything, apparently. I drum my hands on the tabletop.

"What's our strategy?" Meadow asks.

"How about I run around the room knocking everyone's cups down but without saying anything or using any verbal cues?" I say, jokingly. She cracks a little smile.

"Let's start with the base and for each row we go in this direction?" She points to the cups.

"Fine," I say.

"All right, class, focus! Don't worry about other groups, make this round your personal best," Mrs. Graham says.

"But still focus on beating them," Meadow says into my ear.

Has she ever lost anything?

"Guess what?" I say. "I have a good team name for us: Team Not Fast, Just Furious. Works if we win or lose." This gets Meadow laughing. Better. That's what I want our strategy to be.

"Timer's ready . . . and go!" says Mrs. Graham.

We're smoother, faster. We nod and shake our heads and exaggerate our facial expressions to communicate every move. We build our tower . . . until I accidentally knock it over with my elbow. Meadow yelps, but happily. She's still laughing.

"Not fast is right," she says.

We rebuild our tower as fast as we can, but now she accidentally knocks it over with her wrist. We can't catch up, but we're both laughing.

"Time's up," says Mrs. Graham. Meadow and I glance around. Everyone's towers are fully stacked except for ours.

"We did it! We lost!" I shout, and we both let out more laughs. Mrs. Graham walks around the classroom and smiles at us. "Excellent teamwork, you two."

"See? Last place isn't painful at all," I say.

I lay my palm low for a sly victory slap and Meadow playfully rolls her eyes. She reaches out and quietly smacks my hand, this time with a smile.

MAKE IT TO PLAYOFFS

For a whole week now it's been soccer, soccer, and more soccer. Dad's really pushing the whole team. Between all the extra coaching my cousins are giving me and how strong my teammates are, we keep winning, and I keep blocking goals. It's like a miracle. Soccer's still not my favorite—even when I'm blocking balls and everyone's cheering me on, I'd rather be sliming—but Nick was right. I'm more comfortable playing, and everyone's forgotten about that terrible first game.

Sunlight streaks the field as the G-Beatz and I sprint up and down the turf doing drills. After our scrimmage we wrap up with one more drill: Dad stations me at the net and has everyone line up. One by one each player kicks the ball my way as hard as they can. I block them all.

When practice ends Trevor sprints up to me. "You're like our secret weapon!" He pats me on the back like we're total buddies now. "You should come over sometime after practice. You and Logan," he says, before running off to Rudy and the other boys he normally hangs out with. Seems like the more goals I block the more he wants to be friends.

Dad and I walk to the car, mesh bag slung over his shoulder. "Good news, I've been looking at a report of our stats and we just need a few more wins to make it to the playoffs! I'll announce it at our next practice." He pats me on the back and we both smile. "I knew you could do it."

YOU CAN GO ANYWHERE

The day after practice, Trevor invites me over to his lunch table, where he's sitting with Logan and their friends. Logan looks at me like he doesn't want me there. Fine, I get it. Business partners only.

I scan the courtyard and spot Pepper and Carl playing cards and laughing. They don't have any Slimebreaker jobs the way they did for the Slime War. I never even apologized to them. I wasn't being a good friend.

I wave to Trevor and Logan, then walk over to Pepper and Carl.

"Is it okay if I sit here?"

Carl's eyes get big, but he scoots to make room and I set my things down. Pepper looks around at the courtyard, the cafeteria, her lunch bag. Everywhere but at me. But they both put their cards down.

"Why aren't you over *there*?" Carl nods his head toward Logan and Trevor's table.

"If you're still mad, I get it." I grab my stuff to leave.

"I mean, I *was* mad," Carl says.

"We *both* were," Pepper says, and Carl gently nods. "We were ready to help you with the Slimebreaker, but then it seemed like all you and Logan wanted to do was hang out with Trevor, so . . ."

"I know, and I'm really sorry. I'm sorry I got us all caught and that I was ignoring you. I think I was embarrassed by what happened and I didn't know what to say."

Finally Pepper looks up at me. "We forgive you." She cracks a smile and moves over for me to sit. "Besides, some other dumb drama will happen soon and every sixth grader will forget about the Slime War and move on to the next thing."

I smile back and join them. "I hope so."

It's only awkward for a few more minutes before we get back to how things were. They both want to help me win the Slimebreaker, too.

"I was thinking about what you said, wanting to know your customers better? I've got a good tip," Pepper says.

"What's that?" I ask.

"Just talk to them! Ask lots of questions about who they are, what they like, what they hate. It's the best part about having a store," she says.

"Yeah, like whenever I go to the Magic Shop, Marty and Fran, who work the counter, always ask to see my new tricks. And they always remember my name."

I nod, thinking about Lolo and Lola and how so many

customers who've walked into the market started off as strangers but turned into people we know and recognize who have names and tastes and stories. When my grandparents ask them about how their days are going, they truly want to know.

"This is all good millionaire-making advice," Carl says.

"Good friend advice, too," I say, and Pepper and I smile at each other. "If I win Slimebreaker, you're both going to be a part of my new business. Me, you, Pepper, and Logan. Fifty-fifty-fifty-fifty."

Pepper snorts. "All right, but first let's work on your math."

"And don't say *if*, say *when*," Carl says. "Is this yours, by the way?" He pulls a baby carrot stick from behind my ear and offers it to me.

"How are the G-Beatz doing?" Pepper asks.

"We made it to playoffs, our game's this weekend. Can you believe it?" I say, and Pepper flashes me a warm smile.

We keep eating and talking and catching up, asking each other tons of questions. We're not strangers anymore. I feel better now. Lighter. This is what I've been missing.

SO SUCCESSFUL

I walk into my cousins' house without knocking to meet for practice after school. They're already playing soccer but on-screen, wedged deep into the couch shouting at a video game. They're concentrating as much as they would on a real-life match.

Nick scores and punches a fist into the air. "FIFA champion of the wooooorld!" he shouts, and Sammy throws his controller onto the floor.

"Cheater," Sammy says.

"How?" Nick asks.

"Hey, looky who's here!" Sammy yells, and he runs to the door and tackles me.

"I'm getting squished!" I say, laughing, but I defend myself and trick him into a good headlock.

Sammy gets up. "I knew you had it in you, little cuz. Okay, goalie time."

"Hey, guys, instead of doing drills, can we do something else?"

Nick goes to the front door and puts on his cleats. "You want the G-Beatz to make it to the playoffs or not?"

And that's the thing—I do. But I also tell them about Dad's "m market" sign and it makes my cousins laugh so hard.

"Lolo's gonna hate it," Sammy says.

"I don't think so. I talked to Lolo and Lola, and they think we should try things out. But I think we should do some research and check out our competition. We should see why it's so successful, maybe get some ideas for the store." There's a huge Asian grocery not far from our market, and when it first opened a few years ago, it started taking business away from us.

"Can we all go? We can skip soccer today. I'm not completely horrible at it anymore."

They consider my plea and Sammy says, "Smart thinking. You really will buy me my first Lambo."

"On one condition," says Nick, and he points at Sammy. "*He* buys us dim sum."

Sammy smiles at his brother. "I'll buy Alex lunch. You're on your own, weirdo."

"Fine, whatever." Nick turns to me. "But your playoffs are coming and you made it this far, so soccer first."

My dad says compromise is the sign of a good leader in business and in life. I'll take it.

FISH EYES

We always end what Nick calls Cousin Practice with what Sammy calls Pre-Dinner, so it's a good time to go food shopping. As usual they worked me hard, so my stomach grumbles as we drive to the Asian Supermarket—a massive grocery store with the most straightforward name ever.

"Wow, I haven't been here in so long," says Nick. We pause and look up—the building's huge. At the glass doors Sammy waves his hands and says *Abracadabra!*—and they slide open. We're greeted by rows of red shopping carts, glossy floors, and aisles and aisles of every product. Above us: bright lights. Around us: all different kinds of people and families and kids flowing in and out, and I think I hear every different Asian language at once. *And* I already smell something delicious coming from the café.

"I'll grab a cart!" Sammy runs off.

"So, Lil A, what are we looking for?" Nick asks.

I'm not exactly sure yet, but I'm thinking inspiration. "A *feeling*. Ideas. Things we should sell."

"Then let's go!" Sammy returns, balancing on a cart, and he pushes off with a hop forward. We follow behind him.

"Down there!" I point to my favorite section—the longest snack and candy aisle *ever*. Straight out of the best dream. It's packed with chips and sweet things in fun, bright packaging and labels in languages I don't understand. It's a much larger version of what's in our market.

The row is clear of shoppers. Sammy zooms to the huge section of gummies and jellies, and my cousins pull everything out, from lychee-flavored to mango and strawberry, and drop it all into the cart as we keep rolling.

"Fish eyes!" Nick points to the seafood section. As we get closer it starts smelling of seaweed and the ocean. The fishmongers work behind a long, tall counter, and fish piled on ice stare at us with their big glassy eyeballs, which used to freak me out. We stop to look at the tanks full of silvery fish and lobsters with long antennas. It's like a mini-aquarium. There's a basket of small blue crabs clawing around, and a man behind the counter takes some out with tongs and drops them into a paper bag for a customer—I can hear the crabs scratching. One little kid picks up a crab with tongs, too, making it fight with the ones still in the basket until his grandma stops him.

It's chilly walking through the store, and the hair on my arms sticks straight up.

We roam past huge sacks of rice, which we slap; the

produce section with towers of Chinese broccoli; the knick-knack section, with toys that part of me wants to play with even though I'd get made fun of for wanting to do such a little-kid thing. My stomach grumbles some more.

"Dim sum time!" Sammy says.

We point to what we want through steaming glass windows and an auntie in a hairnet piles everything onto our plates. We find a table in the open dining area.

In a room across the way, I notice a group of women—Asian mom and grandma types—at tables with orchids. *Orchids.* Mom's favorite. I set my plate down.

"Be right back."

The room smells damp and sweet. It's an orchid show.

My mom used to enter these shows, too—I've seen lots of pictures, and Lolo and Lola put some of her ribbons in the Shrine. Sometimes I catch Dad taking them out and touching the back where she signed her name.

I walk through and admire the pretty blooms, most of them with price tags on the pots. Everyone's talking, and some of the older women remind me a little of the lolas in my family. It feels like a neighborhood party.

One lady waves me over and offers a sweet, sticky rice cake from a tray.

"Anak, try some," she says. I take a bite-sized square and pop it into my mouth. I will never turn down free Filipino food from a friendly lola.

"Thank you," I mumble with my mouth full. "Lola, what is all this?"

She grins at me. "We hold a show once a month. Do you come to this store a lot?"

I shake my head. "My family has our own store. I'm Alex."

"Alex . . . Manalo?" she asks.

"How do you know?" She gives a gentle laugh and tells me she's friends with my grandparents—of course. "And I knew your sweet mom, too. She always brought wonderful energy to these events, and beautiful flowers."

How cool.

We chat and she offers me rice cakes to take back to my cousins. I do, and after filling our bellies with all the good food, we walk back to the car carrying bags of fun snacks. And suddenly, a brand-new idea is starting to grow.

IF WE LOSE

It's the morning of our Very Important Game—the playoffs. It's all I could think about this whole week. If we win, we're in the finals. And if we win that, I get my first real sports trophy ever, and not just the "hooray you participated but lost!" kind.

Dad's at the Shrine, whistling, dusting, and shifting things around.

"What are you doing?" I ask.

"Making room for the G-Beatz."

"But . . . what if we lose?" I ask.

"We get a medal no matter what, right?" He smiles at me. "Although I'm leaving extra room for a championship trophy, just in case." I squirm a little. "I think you're ready. I *know* you're ready." There's his huge grin again.

"I'm going to take a bike ride," I say.

"Don't be too long. We have to leave in an hour."

I strap on my helmet and head out. It feels good to be

away with the wind on my arms and the sun shining just right.

Through the park of early-morning risers.

Past my school.

A little farther, where big buildings sit on giant parking lots.

One lot has multiple tents with rows of orange traffic cones and people in bright yellow vests directing cars. Signs taped to the light poles say GOLDEN VALLEY FOOD BANK.

I roll by slowly to see what they're doing. Grown-ups are standing behind tables handing out boxes to long lines of people. There are so many people waiting in line, even kids who look my age. I'm wondering about who they are and how they got there when I see Meadow.

She's with her mom at the front of a line, and a man gives them a food box. I ride away fast so she doesn't know I saw her.

At home I rush to slip on my uniform and my socks, but I'm still thinking about Meadow.

"Alex! Let's go!" Dad calls. I help him grab the cooler and the mesh bag of soccer balls and we head out.

A cool wind picks up. It's the kind of clear, crisp day that makes me feel like I can do anything. I smile.

When the season started, playing a sport felt nothing like me. But when I'm with other kids doing the same thing—working together, trying our best, blocking a goal and cheering . . . it does. It's not that different from when my friends and I make slime.

Out on the field, Dad says, "G-Beatz, this is it. You men have been working hard all season. If we make it to the championship, that's fantastic. And if we don't, you've all put in admirable effort." He looks directly at me when he says the last part. "Okay, team, all hands in! One . . . two . . . three . . ."

"We're gonna Beatz you!" we all shout, and sprint out onto the turf.

My arms feel like noodles.

Don't screw up.

Last night Dad said he'd make me goalie for the second half, Trevor for the first. This is huge. Our opponents scored ten to zero in their last game—they know how to score. I'll have to be ready.

Kickoff.

I'm not bad out in midfield, defending and attacking the ball, giving assists to my teammates so they can score. The other team's good, but so are we. When halftime hits we're tied, one to one.

We run off to the side of the field for swigs of water and another quick pep talk before switching off into different positions. The game starts up again.

"Block them," Trevor tells me, and my eyes focus, razor-sharp.

In the end, I block two goals and my teammates score four. The whistle blows. The final score is four to three.

The G-Beatz win!

"We did it!" I shout.

My teammates and I run up to each other. Dad joins us, too, and for the quickest second scoops me up and gives me the hugest hug. The G-Beatz and I jump and shout so loud with a feeling I've never had: of winning, of being a part of something, and of making Dad so happy.

SOCCER DID THAT

I don't want the excitement to end, so once we're home from the match I run up to my room, slam the door, and start pulling every ingredient off the shelf as fast as I can. I want my winning Slimebreaker batch to feel like silk but also have a mega-bounce. Sometimes people think you can't have both—soft and strong—but they don't know what's possible. Just like every ball that hurtled at me but I managed to block—I never thought I could do it. If people could have that shiny feeling—of dreaming, then doing, then succeeding—maybe the things that scare them wouldn't feel that way anymore. They'd see every possibility.

A ping goes off in my head. A buzz. A new plan. One that would help every single kid at my school. Except Meadow would need to agree, and I don't know if that would ever happen . . . I'll have to think on it more, and figure out how to make it really work before I talk to her about it.

I mix ingredients and *shake, shake, shake* a vial of mini-confetti balls to add some interesting texture. They sound like castanets.

"Self, come up with the best slime you've ever made!" I shout.

"Come up with what?" asks Dad.

I jump up and the confetti flies: onto the table, into the carpet grooves, all over my shirt. The door's wide open and Dad's standing there and looking at my bowl of slime.

Oh no.

"Alex, is that what I think it is?"

He steps closer to look and I yank Mrs. Graham's instructions off the wall. "I'm making this for science class! It was assigned!"

He takes the sheet from me and his eyes zip back and forth as he reads through.

"Well, I've been watching you get serious at other things, too, so if this is for school, that's fine. Your teachers know what they're doing."

"Really?"

"Here, I brought you something. I wish I had it for today's game, but you'll have it for the big one." Dad hands me brand-new goalie gloves.

"These look kind of expensive."

"They weren't cheap, but they're good quality and they'll be a good tool. You earned them *and* you paid for them." He smiles.

"I did?"

"Logan's mom split up the money you kids made from your Slime War and gave it to us parents. We changed our minds about how to handle it. Each family is deciding what to do with it."

"You bought something with my money . . . and didn't ask me about it?"

"I think you can take the goalie thing far, Alex. And don't worry, the gloves were on sale. The rest you can save for college, the way Lolo and Lola did with what I earned working at the market."

Dad leaves. I thought for sure he'd get mad about seeing me slime.

Wow. *Soccer did that?*

Imagine how he'll feel once I show him what I can really do with what I really love. Now I *have* to get this batch right.

THIS ISN'T HOW

Another Monday, but not just any morning—the morning after playoffs. Dad and I are sitting at the dining room table over breakfast. He still can't stop gleaming or talking about our victory.

"I dreamt about your match last night, Alex! I can't stop replaying it in my head!" He laughs in a giddy way like we're opening up Christmas presents or something. As we finish eating and start putting everything away, he says, "I was thinking, you've gotten to be such a strong player, we should look for another league for you after the season ends."

"More soccer?" I say.

Just like Dad, I still have a thrill from winning, but it's weird, too. Even though I played my best game ever, I'm . . . kind of over it now. Once we're finished with the championships, I don't know if I want to keep going. This still feels more like his thing than mine.

"Maybe we could try a travel league. How cool would that be? I'll look online later," he says, with his smile still so wide.

"Could we just get through the big game first?" I say.

He nods. "You're right. Way to focus, son." Dad pats my arm and we both head out the door.

When I get to school, Trevor and some of our teammates in the courtyard spot me and wave me over. I join them, everyone talking nonstop about our close game. Even Dad hasn't stopped telling everyone he sees.

"Wait until you see my congratulations present for you," Trevor says to me. When I look at him, confused, he says, "Just wait."

After last period kids swarm the halls. I notice Meadow in the thick of it, and she seems really upset. For a second we lock eyes; then she hooks arms with Kristina B., who tries to comfort her. I wonder what happened.

I head for my locker and spot a plastic bag hanging from it, with the Dollar Dreamz logo. There's a sticky note and I peel it off.

Congrats! Thanks for the win. –T & L

I look around.

Trevor walks past with Rudy. "My gift to you for making playoffs—you saved us a bunch of times! It was awesome," Trevor says. "King of Slime, here you come." He flashes me his winning smile.

"Didn't think you had it in you," Rudy says to Trevor, and he pats him on the back.

Trevor grins back at him. "I'm good like that."

I peek in. The bag's full of glue bottles.

T & L?

Trevor and Logan? They went through with Trevor's sabotage plan? Did Meadow see this? Will she think I did it?

Logan knows this isn't how I want to break the tie.

"Guys, I don't want—" I say, but when I look up, Trevor's gone.

I head over to the bike racks and loop the bag over my handlebars. The bag swings as I pedal off.

WHAT'S YOUR FAVORITE SLIME?

I bike to the park across the street. A wind blows and scatters leaves along the paths. For a while I circle around, searching for Logan or Trevor—I don't want anything to do with their "present"—but no luck. I can't find them anywhere. I'm too mad to talk to Logan now, anyway. I can see Trevor doing something like this, but Logan? They can have their friendship and keep me out of it.

I push off to leave but see Meadow sitting on a bench. Her backpack, the sparkly one—the same one I thought meant she was a different kind of person—sits on the grass next to her. She's crying. I bet I know why.

Slowly I roll up to Meadow, but she doesn't look at me. "Are you . . . are you okay?" I ask.

"Leave me alone, Alex."

"I know we're not friends . . . but . . . sometimes it helps to talk?"

Meadow wipes her face and gives me her scowl, the

one I'm used to by now. "Why are you being nice to me?" she says.

Sheesh. I was only trying to help.

"Why are you always so *mean* to *me*?" I shoot back. Her lip trembles and now I feel bad. I pause. "It's not like we're . . . total enemies, right? Sometimes we're almost kind of like . . . science class friends?" I try to laugh. "Kind of?" *Okay, stop blabbering now, Alex.* I glance at the bag hanging from my handlebars. "Look, do you need supplies? Is that why you're so upset?"

"My mom and I are having a hard time, that's all."

"Do you . . . do you want to talk about it?" I sound exactly like Lola and Auntie now, but Meadow's still crying, and it's a little awkward. I'm not sure what else to say.

"We lost our apartment and we've been staying with family. I've been trying to help, but I don't know how to do that anymore." She wipes her face with her sleeve.

"Oh. Sorry." I remember what Logan told me about her family owning a flower shop. "Did something happen with your mom's business?" I get off my bike and sit next to her now. I think she could use a friend. "Whenever our store goes through hard times my family always gets really worried."

"That wasn't my mom's main job, and it wasn't our store, I just let people think that," she says. "We've had a lot of bad luck lately, that's all. I want to keep sliming, but my mom hates it."

"Does your dad not like it when you slime, too?"

"He's not around anymore, but we're better off without him." Meadow looks away. "It's weird that you asked me about supplies . . . I went to Dollar Dreamz and they didn't have any glue, the lady said they sold out. Has that ever happened to you?"

I shake my head. "No."

She sighs. "I thought if I won Slimebreaker I could help my mom because I could keep selling, but she said it's not my responsibility." Our gazes lock. "You're not going to say anything, are you? Especially not to Rudy or Trevor. They're such blabbermouths."

"I won't. I promise."

I take the bag from my handlebars and place it on top of her backpack. "You should have this."

She peeks inside and is quiet for a long moment. "You just . . . had all this lying around?"

"It's extra. And if you couldn't find glue—"

"I don't need any handouts, Alex." Meadow's tough tone creeps back. "And I'm not asking you to feel bad for me, either, even if it is *extra*."

I shake my head. "I don't think you need any handouts," I say. "I think it's cool you're trying to help your mom."

Meadow looks at me for a long moment, like she's trying hard to figure something out. "What's your favorite kind of slime?"

"Easy!" I unzip my backpack and pull out a sample. She opens it, takes a whiff, pokes in a finger.

"Cotton candy. Nice."

"Have you ever tried baby oil? A few drops will make your slime less sticky and give it that popping sound."

We start bouncing tips around: which kinds of shaving cream make the fluffiest slime, and which lotion gives the most stretch.

She hands me back my slime.

"I have to know something," I finally say.

"What is it?"

"Why'd you save me in Mrs. Graham's class that one day?"

She hesitates. "I felt bad about the video." She looks down at her hands. "I *am* mean, Alex. Everyone says it behind my back. And I was mean to you. I'm sorry."

"That was the worst day," I say. It was.

"People wanted me to do it and so . . . I did. I guess I thought if I helped you out in class we'd be even."

She hands me back the bag. "Here. I'll figure something else out."

"Are you sure?" I say. "If one of us is going to beat the other, we need to do it fair and square, and we both need supplies. And seriously, someone gave all this stuff to me." It's not like I'm lying. I have more than most kids need—for lots of things, I'm realizing.

Meadow studies me the way I do when I don't trust something, but then she says, "Would ten dollars cover it? We can swap tomorrow."

Like a true businessperson, she extends her hand. And like a true competitor, I shake it.

THE ONLY WAY

At home that night I sit on my bed, staring at my soccer uniform. Dad's hung it on the closet door like he can't wait for the championship match to start, even though it's not until this weekend. He's ready—my nerves are not.

I'm glad Meadow and I talked earlier, but it's Logan I still need to figure out. I'm not sure what to do or what to say to him or Trevor.

I plop back and stare at the ceiling. Maybe I should leave it alone.

My bedroom door swings open. It's Nick. He starts bouncing a soccer ball on his thighs while stuffing a cookie into his mouth. He's got skills.

"Let's goooo!" he shouts.

I sit up. "What are you talking about? Where?"

"I told my friends all about you and they want you to play with us. I agree."

Nick spends every waking moment thinking about soccer because it's what he loves more than anything. Tonight he's got a game not for his team but for fun. Most nights he plays with his friends.

"Play with you and a bunch of high schoolers? No way. I'll get destroyed."

"Then just come watch. You can still pick up some good moves before your big match."

"Fine," I say, and we head downstairs. Anything to get my mind off things.

Dad drops us off at a field nearby. It's dusk, and over the soccer field are the brightest streaks of pink and orange in the sky. Makes me think I should create a Sunset Slime one day.

Nick introduces me to his buddies, and they all joke around and seem super nice. They're around his age, maybe some older, and they all look like different kinds of guys, some sporty and some not.

"Let's see what ya got, Alex," one of them says. I'm embarrassed but I play anyway, then finally sit it out. They're so fast and smooth, it's more fun to watch. Soccer's like a powerful dance. Nick and his friends are kicking the ball into the goal with so much force. Every time someone shoots for the net I hold my breath until the ball makes it in.

The game ends, and Nick's friends step off the field. There's another group of players who've been waiting to play.

"Took you long enough," says someone from the other group.

"What's that supposed to mean?" says one of Nick's friends.

"Didn't even realize people like you play soccer," the guy says.

Nick steps in front of those guys. But calmly, he says, "People like *what*?" Nick takes another step forward and I do, too. I don't want anything to happen to him. "This is a public field. Lots of people play soccer here."

The two groups eye each other seriously, like they're daring each other to say something more, but nobody does. Nick's friends walk off and the others walk on.

I take a seat with Nick on a bench as we say goodbye to his friends and wait for Dad to pick us up. Nick watches those rude guys get onto the field and he frowns. It reminds me of those hoodie people who were checking out our market and were acting like they knew it all. I could have said something to them, but I never think of comebacks until it's too late.

Walking toward us I see a familiar kid, and he's smiling. It's Trevor. He's with his dad, who has a soccer ball under his arm, too. They were probably practicing, the way Dad used to make me do with him.

Trevor waves and I say to Nick, "Be right back."

I jog over to Trevor.

"Alex, nice to see you, buddy. I've been watching you at practice. Great improvements," his dad says, and I thank him. "Meet you in the car, Trev."

Trevor puts his hand out for a slap the way I see him do with his friends all the time. "Ready to become champions?" I hesitate and then slap back.

"You know it," I say. "But there's something I need to tell you first."

"Did you like your present?" He gives me a huge smile. "Nice, huh? Thought I'd help my new friend out."

I can't believe that's what he thinks.

I shake my head. "No, it wasn't nice, Trev."

"You want to win Slimebreaker, or not?"

"Sure I do. As much as I want to win the championship tomorrow."

"Then what's your problem? It's not like Meadow can't get supplies someplace else."

"You don't know that," I say. "It's not how I want to win—or lose."

Trevor rubs the back of his neck and glances toward his dad, who's waving him to the car. "I did kind of feel bad after," he says quietly.

"Then why'd you do it?"

"Everyone wanted me to, especially Rudy," he says.

"Who cares."

"Trev, let's go now!" his dad shouts.

233

My eyes meet Trevor's, but he runs to his car.

I join Nick again. "Who were you talking to?" he asks.

"Some kid from the G-Beatz."

Nick nudges my side. "Hey, I'm proud of you on the whole soccer thing."

"Yeah, so am I." I smile. "Thanks for all your help."

"Uncle said you're joining another league after your season ends? Good for you."

I groan. "I never agreed to that."

He turns and looks me in the eyes. "Do you like playing soccer? I mean, I know you've gotten better, but is it something that feels fun for you? Like for me, I can't wait to get onto that field, you know?"

I think of the things I do like about playing, but it's mainly the friends—and the ice cream after. I shake my head. "Nope. Even if I'm better, I still dread every time I have to go on the field."

Nick laughs, hard. "Then what are you waiting for? Tell him."

"My dad? How? He's always so excited, like he doesn't have anything else he can talk to me about. I don't want him to be disappointed."

"He won't be, I promise. Sometimes you have to do things that make you feel uncomfortable. Like I didn't want to talk to those jerks back there, but if I didn't say anything I would have been so furious at myself." He spins the soccer ball on his finger, then catches it. "If I don't speak up for me, who will?"

"That's true. But I was kind of scared something might happen."

"Yeah. Sometimes you just need to say your piece, but also know when to walk away." I nod and he throws the ball to me. We play a bit, and a few minutes later Dad pulls up and unrolls his windows. "You boys have fun?" he shouts.

"Trust yourself, Alex," Nick whispers as we walk toward the car. "Say whatever you need to. You know what you're doing."

WHAT I'VE BEEN HOLDING IN

A whole week has passed. More sliming. More soccer. And now, the big day. This afternoon the G-Beatz play our championship match.

Deep breaths, Alex.

I'm at my desk *still* trying to come up with the perfect Slimebreaker batch. I've been avoiding Logan since he and Trevor left that bag on my locker, but it's fine, I haven't been able to think about anything other than today's game. Goalie's an important position, and I don't want to mess up out there. My cousins have been practicing with me every spare second.

Sammy's voice outside yells, "Nothing but net!" Basketball's his weekend-morning routine. I run downstairs. He's always got good game-day advice, and maybe I'll feel calmer after talking to him.

I close the front door behind me and see Sammy and Nick, except they're with someone. It's Logan.

What's he doing here?

Logan sprints up to me to say something, but suddenly I can't keep inside what I've been holding in all week.

"If you came here to gloat like Trevor about taking all that glue like you did me some sort of favor, you didn't. I gave it all to Meadow," I say. "You and Trevor can do whatever you want, just leave me out of the mean stuff. It's not how I want to win."

As soon as the words leave my mouth it's like I can think again. My head feels clearer.

Logan's face scrunches up. "Wait . . . what? What glue? I came here to wish you good luck on your game." He stuffs his hands into his pockets. "I was going to tell you that Carl and Pepper and I are coming to watch."

"The bag on my locker? There was a note on it with your initials, and Trevor's."

He groans. "I can't believe he went through with it. Trev tried to get me to help, but I said no. Meadow didn't deserve that—nobody does."

"It wasn't you?"

Logan shakes his head. "I almost went through with it, but it didn't feel right. Trev used to make me do things like that all the time. I'd always go along and feel bad after."

"I'm sorry. I thought . . ." I'm not sure what I thought anymore.

"I came here because . . ." Logan's voice trails off. "I don't like how things got all weird. I miss hanging out."

"Yeah. I do, too," I say.

"Sorry, Alex. Trevor's not a real friend, but you are. Or were. Or could be again."

I can see he means it. And just like that we start talking about how we hate it when other people try to force us to do things we don't want, how we don't feel like ourselves when that happens. How I felt angry at him and he felt jealous of me for getting Trevor's attention with soccer. We share and listen, all while my cousins shoot hoop after hoop.

"Hey, can we do something?" I ask.

"What?" Logan says.

I put out my hand for a high five and Logan knows what to do: high five, two fist bumps, exploding fingers, pullback. We start laughing.

Sammy and Nick run over. "You never told me you were buddies, little cuz." Sammy pokes Logan in the shoulder. He tries to noogie Logan, and they can't stop laughing. Logan manages to escape Sammy's grasp to slap Nick's shoulder. Then Nick slaps mine.

"Tag!"

Logan jets off and we all chase each other around the cul-de-sac, running and screaming as loud as we can, and it feels good. Like friendship.

GOOD NEIGHBORS

I've given myself a pep talk, but my nerves are still rattling.

Dad and I drive to the store before our match to drop off a few things for the after-party. We'll celebrate together as a team—win or lose. The new and improved Manalo Market is almost finished, so the G-Beatz will be the first to see it.

"Want to wait in the car?" Dad asks. I nod and he runs in.

I notice Mr. Santiago, Dad's landlord friend who owns some of the buildings around here, standing near the empty storefront by our market.

I felt so much better after being honest with Trevor and Logan. And Nick and Sammy told me to use my voice, too.

I get out of the car. "Mr. Santiago?"

"Hi, Alex, it's nice to see you." He spots my jersey. "Game today?"

"Yup, an important one."

"Well, then I'm wishing you good luck." He smiles.

"Can I . . . can I please tell you something?"

"Sure," he says. "What is it?"

I take a breath and try to straighten out my thoughts before saying anything. "I think I met those robot arm guys you were telling me and my dad about. They were here the other day looking around."

"And did you get some free juice out of it?" He laughs.

"No, but they seem . . ." I'm not sure how to explain.

"Yes?"

"They seem like they wouldn't be good neighbors."

Mr. Santiago's smile fades and he rubs his chin. "Did something happen? Do you need me to discuss anything with your dad?"

"No, nothing bad, just a weird conversation my cousin and I had with them." I describe our exchange and how it made me feel. I should have said something at the time to stand up for our store and for my family, but I didn't—so I'm saying something now.

"Interesting," Mr. Santiago says. "Thank you for sharing that with me."

"Will they be moving in soon?"

"We're still working out the leasing terms, so nothing's final yet. There's a lot that goes into these decisions." He looks at the empty storefront and then back at me. "It was nice to see you, Alex." Mr. Santiago walks back to his car and drives off.

Dad comes out carrying a couple of jugs of water. "Did I

just miss Kevin?" I nod and he sticks the water into the back of the truck. "Okay, buddy, it's showtime! Let's go win it."

On the way to the field my head buzzes from nerves, but also because I'm ready. Never thought I'd be one of those kids playing sports, let alone part of a team about to play in a championship. Dad hums happily to himself. It's his dream come true.

HERE I AM

The Organic G-Beatz versus the Weirdo Grandmas.

Let's go.

Game day has blue skies and bright billowy clouds, the cotton-candy kind I want to dive into. It's a home game, our field, and Dad and I meet everyone suited up in our blue-and-yellow jerseys. We're talking nonstop and bouncing balls on our knees, getting out our nervous energy.

On the sidelines, people gather in chairs and on blankets. My family and friends are out there rooting for us, and I scan the crowd for them. Nick spots me and raises a double thumbs-up. Knowing my cousins are watching tangles me up inside.

Coach has made me goalkeeper in the first half, Trevor in the second.

Dad looks over at me a few times with that huge grin, like he can't believe we made it this far. I tug on my goalie gloves, but my hands are shaking so hard.

My team walks toward our gathering spot, Trevor by my side.

"You nervous?" he asks.

I tell him the truth. "Yeah. Super nervous."

"Don't worry, Alex. We got this," he says, as if we're buddies. "*You* got this."

I'm still bothered by what Trevor did to Meadow, and whenever I think about it, I know what kind of friend I want and what kind of friend I should be. Even though Trevor did that, we're cool now. Out on the field we're teammates, so I make the most of it. We can still work together. And off the field, we can do our own thing.

"Two minutes until kickoff!" the ref shouts.

I try to clasp my hands together to stop them from shaking, even in goalie gloves, and head to my starting place in front of a large netted goalpost. A few deep breaths calm me, but barely.

A whistle blows. The game starts.

For a bunch of weirdo grandmas our opposing team is *fast.* And good. And *huge.* Bigger than any other kids we've played—like they've worked out their whole lives and can lift cars with their pinkies.

My teammates are trying hard and sweating even harder. The ball keeps coming my way. All the action's happening close to my net, and I'm sprinting back and forth, trying to anticipate where the ball will go. One shoots toward me, fast, but I aim and reach wide—and block it. The game goes on and I keep blocking ball after ball. Four of them!

Dad's pumping his fists in the air. Everyone's yelling and cheering so loudly.

I'm doing it.

"Go, Alex!" shouts Trevor, and some of the other boys yell, too.

Both teams keep playing. An opponent who looks like a full-grown man shoots the ball at me, and I leap the way Nick made me practice so many times, but the ball goes in. The Weirdo Grandmas score their first point.

"Nice try, goalie!"

"Good effort!"

"Couldn't have done anything about that one!"

I hear all these shouts coming from the crowd—and from our coach, too.

Another ball flies my way. I reach and dive, but it goes past me and rolls into the net.

Two to zero.

Sweat drips down my face every time the ball comes close to the goal. My ears ring and my heart pounds.

"Hustle, goalie!" shouts a spectator. I want to yell back *I am!*

We keep playing, the ball going everywhere—including out of bounds. My team gets a throw-in and it gives me a minute to breathe.

The game continues, and the other team goes for the ball, dribbling steadily down the field. Trevor charges up to an opponent and steals the ball away. But another kid gets it back, kicking in between Trevor's feet, and Trevor trips and falls—and stays on the ground. Every player takes a knee, kneeling down and stopping the game until we know he's okay.

As Dad and the other team's coach run out to check on Trevor, he slowly gets up and raises his arms like a hero. The crowd cheers. Trevor limps over to the sidelines and the ref blows the whistle.

Halftime.

The score is still two for them—none for us.

Trevor's out for the rest of the game because of his ankle. Dad gives him an ice pack and says, "Alex, you're goalie for second half, too. You're doing incredible. Keep it up." He's talking to the rest of my team, but I've tuned out. I only know I have to keep going until the end—and I will. My nerves won't stop rattling, but I'm not giving up.

Second half starts, and the other team seems even faster—is that possible?—kicking and running with lightning force. But the G-Beatz catch up, zigzagging down the field, defending and assisting and cheering whenever someone pulls a good move. They're so on top of it I've barely had to work this half, which feels okay—it's less pressure and gives me a chance to catch my breath.

Every kid seems so razor-sharp and focused. They live for this sport. After all those goals I blocked, maybe someone might think I'm like my awesome teammates, but really all I want to do is get home and work on my slime.

The speed's picking up, and I try to concentrate again. The G-Beatz score once, twice—we're tied! The game's bound to end soon, but if we're still tied, we'll play overtime until one team scores the winning goal.

Someone kicks the ball out of bounds, and the other team gets to throw it in. One of their players takes control and charges with the ball toward the goal. This is my moment. It's all on me. The same strong, giant player who scored the first two goals of the match is charging my way.

He's getting ready to kick, and I brace myself.

Eye on the ball.

"Do it, Alex!"

"Block it, goalie!"

"Get it out of there!"

Here we go.

The player shoots and I watch the ball the whole time as it flies toward me. I lunge, reaching from my toes to my fingertips to block the ball. But all I feel is a whack as the ball grazes the side of my face and lands in the goal. I stumble to the ground. It hurts. It's hard to get up. So I lie there, holding my pounding cheek.

The crowd starts to cheer but abruptly stops. I roll from side to side and the turf scratches my legs.

Dad runs over. I can see that every player—my team and theirs—takes a knee.

I missed the stupid ball. I bury my face in my hands and start to cry.

Tears wet my cheeks, and I know everyone's watching. In all the games I've ever watched my cousins play, I've never seen them cry on the field like I'm doing now. I'm not sure what hurts more, where I got hit or that I didn't block that goal.

I feel Dad's hand on my shoulder. "You okay, son?"

I want to get up like Trevor, who looked so brave limping off, but I don't know how to do that.

My cheek throbs less. "I'm okay."

I try to wipe my face so no one will see me crying as I finally get up and back into position. The crowd cheers.

The Weirdo Grandmas scored and are winning now, three to two.

"We're good, we've still got time!" Dad shouts. For the remaining minutes we all play our hearts out, but no one else scores.

I had one job.

The other team wins the championship.

Because of me.

AMAZING JOB THIS SEASON

All the G-Beatz and their families shuffle through the parking lot toward the store. Through the big windows I see streamers in every bright color hanging from the ceiling, along with a CONGRATULATIONS! banner, which Auntie said would fit the occasion no matter the outcome. Dad leads the way, looking as depressed as the rest of us, and no one's talking except for a couple of moms saying things like: "You guys made it so far!" or "You really improved this season!"

That's all code for we lost.

Burned.

Creamed.

Toasted.

At least my face has stopped pounding. We put an ice pack on it, but Auntie said I may have a nice, fancy bruise tomorrow. Not as big as the one I feel inside for letting everyone down, especially Dad.

Music blasts from speakers, and I catch Auntie Gina smiling at me from the corner as she turns the volume up. She makes an outline on her face of turning a frown upside down, and I try, for her.

"Celebration sundaes for a season well done, everyone!" Auntie points to the new sandwich bar counter, which she converted into an ice cream celebration station with my five favorite flavors—ube, mango, green tea, taro, and macapuno. There are cans of whipped topping and glass bowls filled with sprinkles and different kinds of candies. I think my cousins may have slipped in some of the jellies we got at Asian Supermarket the other day.

Ice cream makes anything better.

My teammates crowd the counter to build sundaes, and I look around at everyone beginning to enjoy themselves in our bright redone space. Even though I miss the hot bar and Dad's changed a bunch of things, it does feel good in here.

These past few weeks my family put in a ton of work, and it shows. It's more organized and open. There are more tables, a new aisle of gourmet goods, and even some tote bags that Nick and Sammy designed with a picture of Lolo on them holding up a box of rice-paper candy. It does look different in here, but when I close my eyes I only have the same feelings: of home, of my family sticking by each other, and of good memories—sneaking Lolo's free candy with my cousins, Lola and Auntie chitchatting with other customers, and cooking with my grandparents in the back kitchen to get ready for a family party. New ones, too, like the nights Dad and I have spent in here dreaming and figuring things out together.

When I open my eyes I see my teammates having fun, the grown-ups talking, kids goofing off out front, and everyone is friendly like I didn't botch the match.

Someone pats my arm. Trevor. "You played a good game, goalie."

"Thanks, Trev. You did, too." I smile and put out my fist for a bump, which he returns.

Dad calls everyone into the shop and we gather in the new café. He stands in the center with all the families surrounding us.

"Time for medals, Organic G-Beatz!"

Parents hold up their cell phones to record. Strong players like Trevor get praised all season long, but this time, Dad goes around giving short speeches about each team member. There's Cael, who never played soccer before but defended every ball, and Alden, who dribbled the fastest of anyone, and Mark, who made up all our halftime boogie dances, which he did whenever another team would shoot and miss a goal. He made everyone laugh.

After going around the circle, Dad reaches the final player.

Me.

"Last but not least, it's always hardest to be the coach's son. *Always.* You're the most improved, Alex."

I stare at my long socks reaching up and over my knees. I'm super embarrassed with everyone watching and listening. But it's a little bit nice, too. We all worked hard, but as the least experienced, I really think I worked the hardest. I know this isn't the sport for me, but I still feel proud of what I did.

"Thanks, Coach," I say, and he hangs the medal around my neck.

"You had it in you, son—we'll keep trying!" He laughs.

I was starting to feel better, and this is what he wants to tell me in front of the entire team? How about *Good effort, buddy*? How about *Hey, thanks for doing this even though you hated soccer to begin with*?

Auntie glances at me and says, loudly, "Amazing job this season, G-Beatz!" She starts off the applause, and everyone joins their players for hugs and pictures.

Dad kneels down to my eye level and stares at my cheek. "Let's get another look, make sure you're okay. You might have a nice shiner tomorrow."

"Dad, why did you say that?" I ask quietly, amid all the commotion. "I never even wanted to play. I only did this for you." He stands but keeps his eyes on me. "You want me to be like you, but why can't you trust the things that *I* want, too?"

I slip off my award, leave it on the counter, and go to the

back office. Behind me, people are high-fiving and saying goodbye and admiring their golden medals, but they're all a blur because my eyes are wet.

I climb onto the tallest tower of rice bags and let out a huge sigh.

"Where's Alex?" I hear a few kids ask, but I stay where I am until everyone's gone.

A LOT I WANT TO TELL

There's a knock on the door to the back room. "How you doing, mister?" Auntie asks.

I'm still on top of my rice throne. Auntie scoots a chair over to join me. "Your mom would be so proud of you, sweetheart," she says, and kisses my forehead. "You did incredible today—this whole season. Your dad's so very proud."

"No he's not."

She strokes my hair. "How about I ask him to come in? I know he'd love to talk."

"Then why isn't he already here?" She doesn't say anything. "Do you really like the store's changes, Auntie?" I ask.

"I like how it's brought us together. I don't even mind the sandwich bar." She laughs. "Because your dad came up with the idea—lovingly. He wants this place to succeed—for you. For all of us."

"Our dumb new menu doesn't make any sense," I say.

"I agree it still needs . . . some finessing."

"So why can't he see it?"

"Have you told him how you feel?"

I think back, but no, I haven't. I thought he'd get mad. I thought he wouldn't be proud if I didn't go along with his ideas. I thought I had to prove other things to him, first, before he'd hear me.

"No."

"Can you try?" she says. "I bet he'd try, too." Auntie gives me a side hug. "Join us out there whenever you're ready, sweetheart. It's just the family now."

After a few minutes the door creaks the tiniest bit, and then a knock.

"May I come in?"

Dad.

"Sure."

"Any room up there for me?" He points to the column of rice pallets next to mine and I nod. Dad climbs up and sits. We don't look at each other.

There's a lot I want to tell him—but I don't know how.

"Alex, buddy, I'm sorry. I didn't mean to make fun of you out there. You worked hard the entire game. The entire season."

Auntie must have said something.

"Dad, I hate sandwiches."

"What?"

"Your sandwich bar. There's nothing Filipino about it. And this is a *Filipino* market. Why would you put in *turkey wraps?*" I shake my head. "It seems so obvious."

"Is that what this is about?" I nod. "What else?" he asks.

"And I would never hide Lolo and Lola's first dollar. I'd hang it where every person who walked in could ask us the story behind it."

He clasps his hands in his lap. "I . . . I see."

"And if I had a son . . . I would never force him to be what he's not. Like making him play sports when he's scared, or finding other hobbies, or telling him to cut his hair all the time." I'm crying now and I don't try to hide it.

"I see," he says again, quieter.

"And if I had a son I would hug him more." I can't hold it in any longer. I feel everything from the past few months—a new school, not knowing anyone, having no friends, getting made fun of, and doing nothing that I wanted but also everything that I did. It all feels so heavy, like something I can't get out of me fast enough. "I really wanted to win today," I say. "I'm not even scared of the stupid ball anymore, but I still blew it."

Dad wipes my tears and opens his arms wide. I lean in to his hug. "You did win, Alex. You won big."

I look down at my feet.

"You know how proud your mom would be right now? As proud as I am. Prouder, even." He kisses the top of my head.

"I wish she was here with us, she was so good at making everyone feel better."

Dad puts one arm around me, and I rest my head on it. He tells me a story about how when Mom was pregnant, she used to whisper to me in her belly that one day I'd be a dreamer and a doer.

"I wish I knew her," I say. Dad smiles sadly.

"Alex, you're a big dreamer *and* a big doer—exactly like your mom and I always hoped for you. And I'm sorry if I haven't realized that you are your own person." He scoots in a little closer on the rice pallet. It makes a loud crinkly noise that sounds like a fart, and we laugh. "I love you. I'm lucky you're my son."

Dad keeps his arm on my shoulder. We stay like this for just a few minutes longer, but it feels like forever.

BASIC SLIME, WINNING TWIST

1/2 cup of shampoo

1/4 cup of cornstarch

6 tablespoons of water

A few drops of yellow food coloring for a
trophy-like gleam

I lie in bed staring out my open windows at the dark sky.

Dad's at the doorway. "Just saying good night, bud."

During our talk earlier, I told him all about tomorrow's Slimebreaker, and for once he didn't ask me to stop mentioning slime. He said maybe we could find a way to make my slime business real, and we could work on it together.

I get out of bed and reach for a tub of my soon-to-be Slimebreaker batch.

"Wanna try it?" I say. I spent the rest of the night after we got home from the market party getting my final batch ready. It'll never be perfect, but it's still great. I'll be sliming as long as I love it, so I have time.

I dump the golden ball into Dad's palm, and he pulls at it. This one's thick and glossy with a high shine. Dad squeezes and the slime squeaks. He starts laughing like a kid.

"Pretty cool, son." He stretches it wide. It's still slime, but soft and manageable. "Untraditional," he says.

"Thanks. I like dreaming up something out of nothing."

"Like your grandparents."

"Like you," I say. He smiles.

"The things you shared earlier about the sandwich bar? Let's figure it out together, too. You have good ideas."

He asks me more questions, and for the first time I'm not scared to be honest and tell him what I think. I'm listening to myself.

"Dad?" We look at each other. "About soccer? I kept playing at first because of you, but then it was for me. And I'm glad I tried, but I've thought about it so much . . . and I don't want to play anymore."

Winning soccer's one thing, but winning at something I really love, something I can feel deep inside, well, that's what I really want.

He looks at me for a long moment and says, "Okay."

Maybe the more I do this, and the more I start speaking up for myself, the better I'll get. Like soccer. And slime. Like anything.

MAY THE BEST SLIMER WIN

On my way to science class, I find Meadow in the hall. I tap her shoulder. We pause midcrowd and kids part around us like a river.

"You ready?" I ask.

She nods. "You?"

I came up with a plan. It's one that's good for me, and good for every kid. But it can only work if Meadow agrees.

"Can I tell you an interesting idea for the Slime-breaker?" I say. Meadow raises an eyebrow and I catch kids watching us, as if competitors can't also be friends. To avoid any eavesdroppers, I pull Meadow aside and explain everything.

"Wow, you really thought about this," she says.

"It's the best way for us to honor the Slime War."

"Agreed," she says.

"Really?"

"Yeah. Count me in." We both grin, and then we do that

thing where we look away and look all around except for at each other.

"May the best slimer win," I say.

This time Meadow's the one who puts her hand out first, and I don't hesitate to shake it.

JUST LIKE BEING IN SIXTH GRADE

Mrs. Graham's class buzzes with excitement. We've brought in our final projects—slime for all! I'm using the same batch as for Slimebreaker later.

Everyone places a batch on their glossy black station tables while on the board, our teacher writes:

The Science of Slime Day!

"Okay, folks, everyone pass your essays up to my desk, please. Then it's slime time!"

We hurriedly turn in our essays to get to sliming as fast as possible. Everyone has compliments, no one judges, because slime's something fun and easy to play with, and that's what we can all agree on.

Secrets of the Slime, AKA Why Slime Is Awesome

Essay by Alex T. Manalo
First-Period Science, Mrs. Graham

Slippery. Gooey. Oozy.

Perfection.

These are all words used to describe one thing: slime.

But what exactly is slime? Not quite a liquid and not quite a solid. In scientific terms, it is a non-Newtonian fluid.

Here in the school world we play with slime, but in the natural world slime is critical. It helps some animals fight disease, protects them from parasites, and helps them fend off danger. One example is the eel-like hagfish. When the hagfish is threatened, it oozes a chemical that turns the water around it into slime—then watch out, predators, because your gills will get clogged! Scientists have even found that slug slime can be used as a kind of sticky Band-Aid. Cool, huh?

Ultimately, as a student of Golden Valley Middle School, here is what I have learned: slime is fun. It brings different kinds of people together. At first, people might get scared or grossed out by it—just watch any old-timey slime movie where a neon-green goo takes over the world. But slime is playful, sticky, and messy. Just like being in sixth grade. Because slime is life.

HOW I PLANNED IT

"It's happening!"

As soon as the last bell rings, bodies scatter like pinballs, and sixth graders herd to the park by bike and on foot. Logan meets me at the lockers. "Let's go," he says, and we fold into the crowd.

At the park, five tables have the same setup: two judges, a plastic mat, and two tubs of unmarked slime. Melvin Moore does his signature bench hop, waving his arms to quiet everyone down.

"Dedicated slimers, I thank you for your presence. I also hereby declare . . . the Slimebreaker!" Everyone erupts into cheers. Meadow and I stand nearby with Logan and Kristina B.

"Let's get this show on the road!" Logan shouts.

"First, I shall reiterate the rules," Melvin says. "The judges will have equal time—three minutes—to play with each batch of slime."

I got up with Dad's five a.m. alarm and made some last-minute adjustments to my batch until I had exactly what I wanted.

Soft.

Stretchy.

Gooey.

And golden like the sun.

The judges are kids from Westward Middle like our testers from R&D. Janae, Oliver, and Riley are in the crowd, too. Janae sees me and gives me two thumbs-up.

"I shall play for us a very pleasing song as our judges do their thang," Melvin says, taking a speaker out of his vest pocket and tapping his phone. Music blares and he counts down: "In three . . ."

He waves his arms for everyone to join in:

"Two . . . one . . . SLIME!"

The timer starts and the judges get to work, beginning with the blue batch. They stretch and ball up, sniff, bounce, and poke. Some of them look at the other judges, some stand, some sit, and a couple take notes, but each of them stays true and focused.

Eyes on the slime.

"My heart's beating so fast," Logan says to me.

Mine too. I barely manage a nod.

The timer dings.

"Slime down!" Melvin shouts, and the judges do as he says.

He sets the timer again for the yellow batch, and the crowd joins in one more countdown.

Logan wrings his hands. "This feels like forever," he says, hopping from foot to foot.

Again, Melvin's timer dings. "Slime's up!" The judges throw down their slime.

"Finally. The moment of truth," Logan says with a big smile.

Melvin raises a baggie of marbles, gives it a *shake shake shake,* and points to a table with two black top hats. "In front of each hat there is a yellow or a blue dot, corresponding with the yellow and blue slime. Judges, please place your marble in the appropriate hat." He walks around to the judges and they each reach into his baggie to pull out a marble. The judges approach the hats and one by one cast their vote.

The last judge drops in her marble, and Melvin saunters over. He turns his back to the crowd and counts, then jumps back on the table.

"The winner of the Slimebreaker is . . ."

Logan holds up crossed fingers. Melvin lifts a hat and shows everyone the color inside: yellow.

Yellow?

"Yellow!" Logan yells.

I won!

Meadow doesn't look nearly as upset as I thought she would, and Logan can't keep still, he's so excited. Everyone claps and cheers.

"Wait!" I shout. "Hold on!" I hop up next to Melvin.

"Speech! Speech! Speech!" everyone chants, but I take a deep breath.

Melvin puts a finger to his lips. "Quiet, please! Our winner and new territory purveyor would like to have some words."

It's now or never.

I look at Logan first, then the kids. "I forfeit," I say.

"What?" Logan's eyes grow huge.

"I forfeit," I say, louder this time.

Kristina B. turns to Meadow with a huge grin. "We win!"

"Wait, no!" says Logan. "Slimers, I'd like a quick word with my client, please." Logan yanks me down to eye level. "What are you doing, Alex? You worked so hard. *We* worked so hard!"

"Logan, it's all good. Trust me." I turn back to the crowd. "I don't want territory, but I'll share it—with Meadow and with anybody who wants to make and sell slime. Why should I get the monopoly? We all know that's not fair."

"If you forfeit, then Slime Legend Rules names Meadow as your successor," Kristina B. says.

Meadow shakes her head no—then smiles at me. "Except that I forfeit, too," she says to the crowd.

This is how we planned it. And if Meadow had won, we both agreed that the same thing would have happened.

"We hereby open up the territory . . . to everyone!"

ALWAYS MAKE A DIFFERENCE

I won! Well, *we* won. We still can't slime at school, but my friends and I can slime together at home—and everywhere else—and share what we love.

My family's wrapping up the changes at the store. This weekend's going to be a little different. Today, especially.

I bike to Manalo Market. I notice lots of movement in the "for rent" space next to our store—people charging in and out with tools and ladders, and moving shelves and desks. Dad says the new tenants will move in soon. I try to spot the robot arms—maybe I can watch them being installed.

As I roll up, Mr. Santiago is outside shaking hands with two women. Over their shoulders he catches my eye.

"Hold on a quick sec," I hear him say, and he comes over with a friendly smile.

"Sooo . . . do my cousins and I get free juice as a neighborly welcome?" I might as well try to make the most of it.

He laughs and shakes his head. "Not quite. You know,

Alex, I'd had some hesitation about the robot business, but you reminded me of what makes a good neighbor." He gestures to the women. "These business owners are making their voice heard. They're launching a community nonprofit that's quite impressive and I think will be good for the neighborhood. They're thrilled to be taking over that space, and you helped with that."

I did?

"Keep making your voice heard, too. It will always make a difference," he says, and he shakes my hand.

Wow.

When I step inside the market, I see that Auntie and Dad have set up takeout boxes and utensils. Everyone's piling food onto their plates.

"Lunchtime!" Auntie says, and she sets up an easel with a giant notepad.

I fill my plate high. I love lunch meetings.

Lolo and Lola are on video on my dad's laptop. "We've got our tiki drinks." Lola raises her glass and cracks up.

Today we're brainstorming as a family.

We decide that the new hot-bar menu will have sandwiches but with some options, including lots of Asian flavors. For our signs, we're using M MARKET for the hot bar and ordering a new, more modern-looking MANALO MARKET sign for the outside of the store, one that lights up bright at night. The shelves will be filled with Dad's yummy gourmet things, but the Filipino aisles stay the most prominent—the first thing people see when they walk in. The second thing they'll see is a cool mural Francisco is helping us paint, with neighborhood landmarks and faces and a colorful sari-sari store in the middle. And Dad decided we can still give out free treats so we can keep it Lolo-style.

"But that'll stop if you keep eating them before the little kids do." He shakes his finger at me.

We'll have a wall of memorabilia that tells my grandparents' story: their market's first dollar, their photographs of when they first came to the United States, a framed newspaper clipping with the headline *Filipino Market Opens to Great Success!* And when people ask, we can tell them my grandparents' story.

And finally, my favorite part (and my idea): "Neighborhood Days." Once a month we'll invite local makers like Ellie and Francisco, and the orchid show ladies, and my sliming friends, too. I did a survey with customers, online and with handouts, and what everyone likes about Manalo Market is how we bring the community together. The stores around our block thought it was a fantastic idea, so we're all pitching in. And Dad's letting me use some of the money I made from the Slime War to help with the marketing . . . and the rest for my new online slime business! I've got an awesome website and even some preorders already.

We eat and brainstorm as Auntie writes out the ideas and goals that are important to us:

- Build our future from the past.
- Neighbors and community matter.
- Food. Friends. Family. Always remember to honor the taste of home.

EVERYTHING STARTS WITH NOTHING

Clear glue

Store-bought slime activator

Water

Liquid watercolor paint or food coloring,
any and all colors

Beads or other add-ins

Wipes for cleaning up (just in case)

Music, food, fun

At last the day's here. There's a new banner hanging high in front of the store this morning:

WELCOME TO MANALO MARKET'S GRAND REOPENING!

The parking lot fills with booths and neighbors. Our old-but-new store is packed with people buying food and snacks and . . . everything.

Plus there's sliming. Messy, unexpected, beautiful sliming.

"I love Neighborhood Days," Pepper says as she squirts glue into a bowl.

Logan, Pepper, Carl, Meadow, and I have set up a giant table with plastic mats and a buffet of slime-gredients where people can make their own, and Melvin's on a portable stage, playing the accordion as background music. And of course we've laid out some batches my friends and I made ahead of time to sell. Carl swirls shaving cream into a bowl for a few little kids and I try my hand at freestyling again, throwing in a little bit of everything, stirring, listening to my gut. It gels together on the first try.

I've also put out some good old-fashioned flyers for my new business: GOO THE RIGHT THING. I make it, sell it, and share slime secrets, but like Lolo said, it's not something for nothing. And he's right. When I put out what I love, I get things back: friendship, awesome ideas, bright feelings. I'm not a legend yet, like Slime Time Soraya, but it's a good start. The other day Raj and I played online and talked—we hadn't in so long. He shared more about how school was going and the new friends he'd made, and I was so happy for him. And I told Raj all about the Slime War and the Slimebreaker and the G-Beatz—and he was super proud of me.

Melvin Moore snaps his suspenders, clears his throat, and shouts:

"To the park, Slimers!"

The sun's high and the sky's so blue. Everyone looks at each other and we jet down the block.

"Alex! Come on!" someone shouts. I can't tell who since we're running so fast.

Kids chase each other, yelling and laughing so loud, it's like the best soundtrack. I hop onto an empty swing, take some steps back, and launch myself with a flying start. Around me I hear my friends' happy shouts, and inside me I hear my own voice, there whenever I need to use it.

I pump my legs to go higher and higher until my feet kick the sky, and I think about how we played a great championship. My friends are still bummed we lost, but that's not how I see it. Now I know how sweet it feels to win.

* * *

After the event it's only me and Dad in the middle of our old-but-new store. I finish wiping down the counters and he grabs our things, whistling.

"What an amazing day," he says with a giant smile. I smile back. "Ready to go? I'll hit the lights."

"I'll get the sign."

We still have a little more work to do around here, but it's nothing we can't handle, and nothing we haven't done before.

I run to the door and flip the sign from OPEN to OPEN AGAIN TOMORROW.

ACKNOWLEDGMENTS

As with *The House That Lou Built* and *Any Day with You,* there are elements of *How to Win a Slime War* that were inspired by my childhood. My family shopped at Filipino and Asian markets, my cousins taught me many things, and, like Alex, I feared sports! But also like Alex, I learned to appreciate and lean on all the different parts of my community to get me through anything.

As I wrap up this novel, our world is in the middle of an unprecedented time. Reading and writing books full of joy and hope are what's getting me through, and I'm lucky to have many people who've helped make this book possible, and to whom I'm sending much gratitude and admiration (imagine big red hearts flowing like a river all over this section):

My editor, Dana Carey, for your brilliance, care, and equal love of puns! (Almost equal? I might outweigh you here. . . .) I'm very grateful and excited to be collaborating with you.

Wendy Lamb for your continued thoughtfulness, keen eye, and surprise fun phone calls!

My agent, Sarah Davies, for your steadfast guidance on this most rewarding journey.

Art director Katrina Damkoehler and illustrator Nicko Tumamak for this book's beautiful and joyful cover.

Managing editor Tamar Schwartz, copyeditor Barbara Perris, and everyone at Random House Children's Books who has helped bring this book to life. Also a massive thanks to the lovely RHCB School and Libraries team for your support and enthusiasm, and for helping me to connect many wonderful educators to Alex's, Kaia's, and Lou's stories.

Authors Alex Giardino, Victoria Piontek, Rachel Sarah, and Kelly Yang for your encouragement, commiseration, and friendship—especially while I was finishing this book during a pandemic!

My longtime friend and go-to for fictional commercial real estate questions, Julie Vieillemaringe Gutierrez.

Youth librarians Cathy De Leon and Cristina Mitra for your thoughtful read.

My three hearts: Mark, Alden, and Cael—I love you! And on behalf of my sons, I'm giving a special shout-out here to Bubbie, Mochi, Ube, Popcorn, Yogi, Crash, and Riggs. (If you're a kid reader who's attended any of my author visits, these are my family's sweet pet ratties and puppy whom you've seen pictures of and have asked many questions about!)

Lastly, to you, the reader. Alex Manalo reminds me of so many awesome kids I've met at schools and libraries around the country with your big ideas and great energy—thank you for inspiring me. Keep reading, writing, and being a part of your community. And, like Alex, keep sharing your joy!

A warm, tender story about a creative girl who hopes that by winning a filmmaking contest, she'll convince her great-grandfather to stay by her side.

Any Day with you

MAE RESPICIO

Turn the page to read an excerpt.

I sit at my vanity with jars of brushes and sponges and a tray of little pots of eye shadows, spread out in a sea of different colors. Today I'm learning a new technique: the ombré effect. That means blending light to dark, or dark to light.

Lainey and Tatang have both been gone for nearly two weeks, and I can't wait for them to see how much better I've gotten.

I press a stencil of fish scales to my cheek, dip a triangle sponge into a shade called Shiny Shamrock, and dab it over the scalloped pattern so that my tan skin warms the green. I do the same thing along my temples and forehead in Misty Aqua. My dark eyes shine against the bright colors.

Last year a few girls in sixth grade started wearing lipstick and blush to school. My parents wouldn't let me do that even if I wanted to. But they don't mind this kind of makeup. It's more like art.

When I was a little kid, whenever someone asked "What do you want to be when you grow up, Kaia?" I always had a different answer:

An artist like Dad. I'm not as good, but I've always loved to draw.

A chocolate-cake tester—someone who eats chocolate cake for a living. I don't know if this actually exists, but it would be the world's best job if it did.

A Sirena. A Filipina mermaid. Part human and part sea creature, a beautiful and powerful guardian of the ocean.

I know now I can't be a real live mermaid, but it turns out I can transform anyone into a fanciful creature with a pop of color and my imagination.

Dad works as a digital effects artist at a movie studio, and there's a whole department there for special-effects makeup. That's a job I want one day. I've been using different characters from Tatang's old tales to practice.

I apply the final dusting of glitter with a fat brush. Sunshine pours in and makes my cheeks shimmer.

Not bad.

"Kaia! Kaia Santos!" a voice shouts from outside. I run to the window. Trey leans on his bike, grinning and waving. "Kaaaaiiiiiaaaaaa Santoooooooos!"

"Want to come up?" I yell back. "I'm mermaiding!"

Trey looks both ways and jets across the street. Then, his usual entrance: the doorbell ringing twice, a quick hi to Mom, his footsteps galloping up the stairs to my door, which flies open.

"Let me see." Trey throws himself onto the bed and I jump up next to him. He flashes the biggest smile. "Awesome."

"Glad you like it, because you're up next."

Trey lets me test out different looks on him. He doesn't normally wear makeup, but he's used to wearing it for theater productions, and maybe he'll put on the occasional guy-liner for fancy occasions. He wants to act one day. Both of his parents are pharmacists, and at first they didn't want Trey to love acting so much—they wanted him to be into *their* hobbies—but now it's his dad who starts every standing ovation at Trey's plays. Sometimes Trey gets to skip classes to go on auditions, which happens a lot at our middle school since everyone in LA wants to be famous (even our plumber, says Dad). Trey's a natural. He can cry on cue without eye drops.

I pull up a chair and throw him a leg from a bright blue fishnet stocking I've cut up. He yanks it over his head so that it covers his face. The holes act like a stencil, and they make a crisscross pattern against Trey's dark skin. He looks like some kind of weird performance art.

"Name your look: Glitter Dots, Magical Merman, or Merman Zombie?" I say.

"Hmmm...Hint of Merman."

I give him the jar of brushes to hold while I work my magic. When I'm done I peel the stocking off and admire the result: a soft pattern of diamonds blending into his cheek like they're part of him.

"Reveal time!" I reach for Dad's old Polaroid camera and point it to face us, and we give our best mermaid grins.

Click!

The camera spits out a square. Trey grabs it and waves it around to air-dry.

"Gimme!" I yank it away and we hunch over the image.

Us, only shinier.

I search my wall for an open space in the growing mass of practice photos. My gaze lands on one of Mom and Lainey made up as mystical engkantos, Philippine nature spirits who live in seas and rivers and forests and can bring good or bad luck. We did this one right before Lainey left. I really miss her. Lainey gets me. Trey and our other best friend, Abby, wish they had a big sister like mine.

Trey glances at his phone. "Hey, Abby's at the Promenade. Want to go find her?"

"But we've never gone out in public like this."

"So? We'll be the coolest merpeople on land!"

He's right. If I'm going to become famous at this I need to start showing more people my art.

"Sure, let's go ask my mom."

Trey holds up the picture. I tear off some tape and pat it into place on my wall, trying to make it stick.